The BLACK Stallion
and Satan

The Black Stallion's colt, Satan, was a great horse. He had won many famous races.

Then from far-off Arabia came the Black—to start the greatest controversy racing circles had ever known. Which horse was faster? Could the speed possessed by the Black, a desert-raised stallion, be matched by his colt, who had been trained solely to race?

Readers will thrill to the terrifying race which brings these two horses together . . . a contest run against the background of a flaming forest fire.

Books by
WALTER FARLEY

The Black Stallion
The Black Stallion Returns
Son of the Black Stallion
The Island Stallion
The Black Stallion and Satan
The Black Stallion's Blood Bay Colt
The Island Stallion's Fury
The Black Stallion's Filly
The Black Stallion Revolts
The Black Stallion's Sulky Colt
The Island Stallion Races
The Black Stallion's Courage
The Black Stallion Mystery
The Black Stallion and Flame
The Black Stallion Challenged!
The Black Stallion's Ghost
The Black Stallion and the Girl
The Horse-Tamer
Man o' War

*All titles available in both paperback
and hardcover editions*

The Black Stallion and Satan

by WALTER FARLEY

RANDOM HOUSE NEW YORK

Library of Congress Cataloging in Publication Data

Farley, Walter
The black stallion and Satan
New York, Random House [1949]
1. Title   PZ10.3.F22Blk   49-6117
ISBN: 0-394-80605-0 (trade hardcover)
       0-394-90605-5 (library binding)
       0-394-83914-5 (trade paperback)

For Pam

Contents

Triple Crown

1

Alec Ramsay sat still and straight in his saddle, seemingly unaware of the thousands of eyes upon him. He wore black racing silks, and beneath his peaked cap the whiteness of his face made a startling contrast to his racing colors and the burly black horse beneath him.

They were third in the parade to the post for the running of the classic Belmont Stakes. Alec wished they had drawn an outside position instead of the number 3 slot. He didn't like being so near the rail. Henry's instructions were to hold Satan until the field approached the middle of the backstretch before making his move. It would have been easier to do this from an outside post position.

The parade had passed the clubhouse and was now opposite the grandstand. Alec didn't have to look to know that it was overflowing with people. The tumultuous roar from the stands took care of that. And he knew their eyes were upon

Satan, wondering if the big three-year-old would win the Belmont Stakes, as he had won the Kentucky Derby and the Preakness, to take his place among the few great horses of the turf who had captured the Triple Crown! They wondered only because of the condition of the track. It was ankle-deep in mud after a heavy morning rain, and the early June sky was still overcast as a fine drizzle fell.

The last remaining doubters of Satan's greatness asked themselves, "But can he race in the mud? He never has, you know."

Alec's hand went to the thick, muscular neck of the colt as Satan sidestepped quickly to the middle of the track. He spoke to him, and the heavy ears swept back at the sound of his voice; then the restlessness left Satan's giant body and he was back in line as the field continued parading past the stands.

From the pushing, heaving wave of people at the rail, a man shouted, "Hey, Ramsay! You think it's a horse show?"

Alec heard the man's words, but his eyes never left the muddy track which he could see between Satan's pricked ears.

"A Good Hands class maybe?" the man called again.

Only then did Alec Ramsay become aware that he was sitting much straighter in his saddle than the other jockeys. The whiteness of his skin gave way to a sudden flush of color, but his seat remained unchanged. He couldn't have sat his horse any other way.

"Bring him home, Alec!" someone else shouted. "Bring him home like you did in the Derby an' the Preakness!"

The post parade ended when they had filed past the stands, and Alec allowed Satan to go into a slow gallop. He rose in his stirrups and leaned forward, his face pressed close to the colt's bulging neck.

Henry had said Satan could race in the mud as well as on a dry track. Henry should know, for he had been training Satan all winter and spring, while Alec had spent most of his time in school. Henry said they had worked Satan in all kinds of weather and the big-boned colt didn't know the difference between a dry track and a wet one. Alec had to take Henry's word for it. He'd raced Satan only twice this year, once in the Kentucky Derby and again in the Preakness. The track had been dry and fast for each race, and Satan had had no trouble winning by many lengths.

He took the big black colt to the outside rail and went past the two horses in front of him. He let him go far around the turn, finding reassurance in the ever-lengthening and confident strides of the colt as he galloped fetlock-deep in the mud. And Alec thrilled to the swift and thunderous movement beneath his knees. But finally he rose still higher in his stirrups and drew back on the reins until Satan had slowed to a prancing crabstep.

He turned the colt to find the others already on their way back to the starting gate, now set in front of the grandstand. He kept Satan to a slow trot, and his hand slid down the thick neck before him. High above Satan's craned head, Alec saw the many cameras set up on the top tier of the grandstand; they were trained on the field as it went to the post.

"Easy does it, Satan," he said as one of the starter's crew took hold of the bridle. Prancing, pulling a little, Satan moved inside the gate. The door behind them was closed; there was only one way out of the stall now.

For a moment, there were the heavy thuds of hoofs

against stalls and the soft whisperings of jockeys to their mounts; all accompanied by the loud, shrieking clamor from the crowd, awaiting the break. Then, very abruptly, a heavy silence fell over the great stands, a silence which finally descended to the starting gate.

Only Satan's big ears moved. Restlessly they pitched forward, then came back until they were flat and heavy against his head. Alec felt the tenseness of the giant colt beneath him. Close to Satan's head he whispered to him. The break would come any second now, any second and they would be off.

"A mile and a half this time, Satan," he said softly. "It's a little longer than the others. Plenty of time for you. Easy getting away, Satan. Easy now . . . wait for me."

The grilled doors clanged open; the starting bell rang. There was an outcry from more than fifty thousand voices that was quickly pommeled to deadening silence by racing, pounding hoofs.

Satan broke with the others, took two fast strides and stumbled! Alec felt his head go down, gave him more rein, then drew back, helping Satan to recover his feet. There was a sickening second of sliding, thrashing hoofs seeking foothold in the mud. Satan's strides came fast and short as he tried to control the hurtling momentum of his heavy body over the slippery track. Alec felt the straining of the great muscles beneath him. He was afraid to move lest he offset Satan's balance still more. He gave the colt his head, yet Alec's hands on the reins were ready to help Satan when he needed it.

Satan's strides were unrhythmical as he plunged forward, but Alec knew the worst was over. The big black colt had gathered himself and his feet were firmly beneath him once more. Even now his strides were lengthening, his body leveling out.

Only then did Alec become conscious of the heaving, sleek bodies to the front and side of him. The start on the muddy track had been difficult for all the horses, but now each was in his stride and moving fast.

Satan's head was pushed forward and he was pulling. Bending low to the side of the black neck, Alec drew back on the reins. "Not yet, Satan. Not yet," he called.

Driving hindquarters rose and fell in front of them, sending mud into their faces. Satan didn't like it, but he didn't attempt to free himself from Alec's tight rein.

The three leading horses swung into the first turn, followed by Satan and the rest of the field. Alec saw the jockeys on his right starting to close in on him; they wanted to bring their mounts into the rail ahead of Satan going around the turn. Momentarily he gave Satan more rein. The colt surged forward, keeping the rail. But the others held on, pressing Satan as he sped about the turn.

The leaders were four lengths ahead as Satan came into the backstretch. Alec took a firm hold, keeping the black colt just to the fore of those running behind him.

"Make your move in the middle of the backstretch," Henry had said. "Not before then. It's only the gray you have to worry about, and he'll be back with you, biding his time."

The gray colt was behind him, as Henry had said. Alec could see his head coming up close beside them. He gave Satan a little more rein to keep ahead of the gray.

The leaders, having spent their early speed, were dropping

back, and Satan bore down upon them with giant strides. But the gray was still pressing the black colt. Together they passed the tiring horses who had set the pace. Together they swept by the half-mile pole and drove toward the far turn.

No mud flew in Alec's face now. The track ahead was clear of horses and only the racing gray, moving at Satan's hind-quarters, could keep the black colt from winning the Triple Crown!

"Now, Satan!" Alec shouted into the wind.

He moved forward and the white rail went by with ever increasing speed. Alec bent low, lost in the colt's heavy, flowing mane. Nothing could stop Satan now, for he was running free, and there was a savage wildness to his action.

For only a few yards did the gray match Satan's tremendous strides. Then he fell back before the fresh onslaught of speed and power displayed by the black colt. And as Satan rounded the turn in all his fury and came down the home-stretch, the eyes of the crowd were on him alone. He was all power, all beauty as he swept beneath the wire, winner by a dozen lengths and the first undefeated Triple Crown winner in turf history!

High on the roof above the stands, a man kept his camera on Satan until the black colt was brought to a stop far up the track; then, turning to another cameraman, he said, "Never in my life have I seen a horse run like that. Never."

"I have," the other returned. "But only once. He was the Black, the sire of this colt. Alec Ramsay was up on him, too. That kid's life is like something out of a movie," he concluded, shaking his head.

"Why?"

"You mean you don't know his story? Where've you been?"

"In Peru, shooting Inca ruins for the last five years."

"Oh."

"What's the story?"

"Alec Ramsay and the Black were the lone survivors of a shipwreck, and the kid brought him home. It turned out that Henry Dailey, the old trainer, whom everyone had just about forgotten, was a neighbor of Alec Ramsay. And when Henry saw the Black he knew what the kid had hold of. They kept the Black in what's no more than a back lot over in Flushing; then they sprung him in that big match race that was arranged for Sun Raider and Cyclone a few years back, and he whipped them both. I saw him do it. It's the only time he raced, but I'll never forget him." The cameraman turned toward the track and Satan. "They could have been one and the same horse today," he added.

"But what happened to the Black?"

"As I heard it, an Arab chieftain by the name of Abu Ishak turned up not long after the match race and proved the horse was his. So he took the Black back to Arabia."

"And that's the end of the Black?"

"It is, as far as I know."

"But where does Satan come in? How did Alec Ramsay get hold of him?"

"The story goes that this Abu Ishak promised the kid he'd send him the first foal by the Black. He kept his promise. Satan is that foal."

"What a break for the kid."

"Yeah. He and Henry Dailey raised Satan in the same lot where they'd kept the Black. They brought him out in the Hopeful last fall. You know the rest . . . he hasn't been beaten yet."

"From back lot to undefeated Triple Crown champion,"

the other cameraman mused, as he turned to the winner's circle, where Alec Ramsay sat on Satan amidst a crowd of photographers. "He's riding high in the big time now. No more back lots for Alec Ramsay. Lucky kid!"

Lucky Alec Ramsay?

2

Alec Ramsay closed the door of the jockeys' bungalow behind him, muffling the shrill voices which rose above the hiss of showers. Standing on the porch, he looked across the wet and empty courtyard to the hoof-furrowed ground of the paddock's walking ring. And his gaze stayed there while he slipped his long arms into the sleeves of his raincoat and drew the belt about him. Then he went down the steps into the steady drizzle.

As he walked to the gate in the iron fence, his hatless head was tucked deep within his coat collar, so he did not see the tall, solitary figure that stood in the rain awaiting him.

"Alec," the man called, as the boy stepped outside.

"Dad! I thought you and Mother would be over at the barn with Henry."

"Mother's there," his father said. "She sent me with this." Casually he lifted an unopened umbrella.

Alec turned from it to the water dripping from the rim of his father's hat. "Why aren't you using it, then?" he said with a smile. "You must have been waiting a long time."

"Never did like them. Do you want it?"

Alec shook his head. "We can put it up before we get to the barn," he said.

They walked past the empty stands, and only the litter strewn about gave evidence of the thousands who had occupied the seats an hour ago. The lights gleamed fuzzily in the rain.

"I don't need to tell you that it was a great race, Alec," Mr. Ramsay said. "A truly great one. He's unbeatable." He put his arm across the boy's shoulders as he turned to him, smiling.

Alec's head was down, his eyes on the wet pavement. "Satan never makes a wrong move, and will do anything you ask of him," he said in a low, even voice. "Henry has done a wonderful job training him, Dad. Satan will go for anyone now . . . anyone who will just sit there and tell him what to do. He's come a long way since . . ." Alec stopped without finishing his sentence.

Mr. Ramsay's face sobered. "You've done your part making him what he is today," he said quickly. "Don't you forget that, Alec—not for one moment. He was a pretty bad colt before you taught him to have confidence and trust in human beings. Henry's gone on from where you left off. He's made a superb racing machine of Satan, but always remember he couldn't have done it without your help."

"Sure, Dad," Alec said. "I'll remember."

They had passed the stands, and their eyes now turned to the long rows of barn sheds a short distance away. They could see the grooms walking their horses under vivid-colored cooling sheets.

"How'd Mother take the race?" Alec asked as they walked down the road.

"Fine. Just fine, except for Satan's stumble at the break. But she came out of it as well as he did. And when the race was over I heard her telling the people sitting next to us that your hands kept Satan on his feet. She's getting to be quite a racetracker, Alec," he added proudly.

As they neared the sheds they saw the crowd gathered in front of Satan's stall.

"The photographers are still here, I see," Mr. Ramsay said. "And there's Mother with . . ." He stopped, and hastily put up the umbrella. "I almost forgot," he said, winking at Alec.

The photographers left the shelter of the shed's roof when they saw Alec Ramsay. They took pictures as he came toward them. They had him stop and asked Mr. Ramsay to put his arm around him, to put the umbrella back a bit, to smile. They took more pictures; then someone called Mrs. Ramsay.

She came through the crowd at the insistence of a photographer: a small, plump woman with a very round face. Her eyes were a little bewildered, but she smiled bravely at Alec and slipped over beside him, holding his arm close to her. She faced the camera, but the photographers told her to look at Alec instead.

"You, too, Mr. Ramsay. Look at Alec and smile. Make it real homey. You're the proud parents. There, that's it. Just move the umbrella over a little more, Mr. Ramsay. Cover the missis. She's getting wet." And everyone laughed.

Then the photographers took pictures of Alec and Henry together. They were very much alike, these two. They made a good picture, and the photographers knew it. They were the same height. Each carried his weight in his shoulders, chest and arms. Henry was heavier through the waist than Alec and his legs were bowed and not so slender, but they could have been taken for father and son.

"Move closer to Alec, Henry," a photographer called.

Henry grunted, pulling his soggy hat far down over his wrinkled brow. "You oughta get out of here," he told Alec. "You've had more than enough for one day."

"Smile as if you were glad to see him," a photographer yelled to Henry. "And push your hat back so we can get a look at your face."

Henry pulled his sober face into a grin, but he didn't touch his hat. "Take your mother and father and get going. I'll follow in a few minutes. I've got my car here."

Alec turned to Satan's stall, where he saw the colt being fondled by one of the grooms Henry had hired. Satan had his head raised above the door, and the perfectly shaped white diamond in the center of his forehead stood out prominently against his black face. Looking for a carrot, the colt shoved his muzzle into the groom's shirt pocket; then more people moved in front of the stall, blocking Alec's view of Satan.

"Don't turn your head away from Henry," someone shouted to him.

"I'd like to be with Satan a few minutes before I go, Henry," he said.

"*Hold it!*"

"They'll follow you in there with him," Henry replied. "It won't be no better for you. You'd better go. Satan's all right. Don't worry about him."

Alec's face clouded. "It's not that I'm worried about him. It's just that . . ."

"Grin, Alec, will you?" the photographers called to him.

Alec grinned and the clicks of shutters followed; then Henry had him by the arm and was taking him up the row to where his father's car was parked. He saw that his parents were already inside.

He sat in the back seat and was quiet as his father drove out the barn gate and headed for home.

It was a little less than an hour later when they arrived in Flushing. The sky to the west was brightened by the glow of New York City lights, and the tall skyscrapers could be seen pushing their fiery towers into the night.

Mr. Ramsay drove down quiet suburban streets and finally came to a stop before a two-story brown house. "The rain is over," he said, getting out of the car.

Mrs. Ramsay followed him up the walk to the house. She had reached the porch when she turned to find Alec crossing the street. She was about to call him when her husband took her by the arm.

"He probably wants to go to the barn for a few minutes, Belle. I'd leave him alone."

"But nothing's there . . . just Tony's old horse."

"He knows that," Mr. Ramsay said, moving her across the porch. "He knows it very well."

When they opened the door, a small dog with shaggy brown hair leaped outside and rose, clinging to their legs with his forepaws. Mr. Ramsay reached down to pull gently on the long ears. "You'd better go with Alec, Sebastian," he said. "I think he'd like to have you around."

The dog stood still before the closed door, whimpering and with his head cocked; then he turned and saw Alec. With a short bark he ran down the steps and across the pavement until he came to a sliding stop before the boy.

Alec bent down to him, holding the soft body in his arms, but after a few minutes he straightened and went to the high, iron-barred fence. Opening the gate, he went inside, followed closely by Sebastian.

The graveled driveway led to Henry's house and one of the few open fields left in a fast-growing area; it stretched before him, coming to an end at an old barn a hundred yards away. Alec walked toward it, his eyes leaving the darkened barn only for the wooden fence to the left of the barn and to the field beyond . . . the field where the Black—and, later, Satan—had grazed.

Reaching the barn door, he opened it and went inside. Even before he switched on the light there was the soft whinny of a horse. Sebastian's feet pattered over the wood floor as he made his way toward one of the two box stalls in the small barn.

Blinking his eyes in the sudden light, a horse pushed his gray, almost white, head over his stall's half-door. Alec went to him, placing his hand upon the soft muzzle. For a moment he stood there, his eyes running over the well-groomed coat.

"Tony takes good care of you all right, doesn't he, Napoleon?" Alec's gaze turned to the cloth hanging on the peg beside the door. "But I guess it wouldn't do any harm to go over you once more." Taking the cloth, Alec went inside and ran it across Napoleon's swayed back. But the horse turned to him, seeking the boy's face.

"Stand still, Napoleon," he said, taking the old head and pressing it close to him.

Sebastian entered the stall, running between the horse's legs and beneath the heavy hanging girth. Napoleon lowered his head, inquisitively watching the dog.

When Alec had finished grooming Napoleon, he went to the water pail and found it full. But he emptied and refilled it; then he got some clean straw and spread it over the floor.

It was only when there was nothing else to do that he turned to the other box stall. He looked at it for many minutes before going to the tack room at the far end of the barn, and there he sat down on a low, flat chest and buried his head in his hands.

"You've got to grow up," he told himself angrily.

When he raised his head again, it was to look at three pictures hanging on the wall before him. They were of Satan. One had been taken when he was a weanling and stood on long spindled legs; another when he was a yearling and already bigger-boned and more burly than his sire; and the last picture was one of him as a two-year-old, standing in the winner's circle after he had won the Hopeful last fall. That had been the beginning of his meteoric career on the track and the end, Alec knew, of having Satan for his own.

There was another picture, larger than the others, on the wall to Alec's left. Without turning to it, he saw every detail in his mind. It was a photograph of the Black's head. Alec had taken it one day long ago, and his father had had it enlarged and framed for him. The background was nothing but sky, and the Black stood out against it so vividly that it seemed you could reach out and touch the finely drawn muzzle, to feel it soft and quivering beneath your hand.

It was a small head, noble and arrogant, with eyes large and lustrous, burning with fiery energy; his silky foretop and heavy black mane were swept back, for there had been a strong breeze that day; his small ears were pricked forward,

almost touching at the tips; and his delicate nostrils were dilated, for he had been suspicious and wary of the camera.

Alec closed his eyes, shutting out the Black's picture from
his mind. But he opened them almost immediately, startled
by the sound of his own voice as he said loudly, "Today I
rode Satan to the Triple Crown championship. No one
could ask for more than that. No one should. I'm the luck-
iest and happiest kid in the world."

He repeated his words to himself, then rose to his feet,
knowing well that he was only kidding himself. He wasn't
happy at all.

The Way It Was

3

Alec was leaving the tack room when the barn door opened and Henry came inside. Sebastian barked and ran to meet him.

"I saw the light and figured it was you, Alec. Anything wrong?"

"No. I was just checking up on Napoleon."

Walking over to the old gray, Henry said, "I'm glad school is about over. Now you'll be able to get to the track mornings with me."

Alec stood beside Henry, his hand on Napoleon's muzzle. "It seems so right to be in this barn, where everything started," he said quietly. "I know we can't keep Satan here, but I wish we could."

Henry turned to him quickly, his face puzzled. But then he smiled and said, "Yeah, it's different at the track all right. The photographers got me down today, too. But you'll find it's not so bad early mornings, Alec. 'Course there are always people around watchin' every move we make with Satan. But you'll get used to it, an' we got no right to expect anything else now."

"No, we haven't," Alec said slowly. "And it's what we wanted."

Henry looked at Alec for a long while before asking, "And now you don't want it?"

"I didn't say that, Henry."

"No, y'didn't. But I got the idea that's what you meant." Henry paused. "Didn't you?" he asked.

Alec turned away, and it was several minutes before he said, "I don't know what I want any more, Henry. I seem to be all mixed up."

"Maybe you oughta talk about it, Alec. We always have. We've never kept anything from each other, have we?"

"No."

"Well, then?"

Alec turned to him. "Sometimes, Henry, I think of myself as a baby who's had his pet toy taken away from him," he said angrily. "I guess I'm unhappy because I can't have Satan to myself any longer. I tell myself to grow up, that I can't make a pet of a champion. I put all the cards on the table. I say this is exactly what I wanted. I'm glad Satan is everything we thought he'd be. I knew from the very beginning that, if he was to be a champion, I'd have to share him with others. I knew his training would have to go on, even though I couldn't always get to the track to ride him. I knew other fellows would be up on him when I wasn't. Everything made sense . . . everything was just the way I'd figured it was going to be." Alec paused, his gaze leaving

Henry for Napoleon. "Yet I'm finding it hard to take . . . much harder than I ever thought it would be."

"Hasn't riding Satan in the big classics made up for a lot, Alec?" Henry asked.

"No . . . not even that. I feel that I'm just a jockey, and I want to be more than that . . . much more." He turned to Henry again, his eyes searching. "It'll be different this summer, won't it? I'll stay with him all the time, and I'll take care of him, too, Henry. We won't need any grooms. . . . There'll be just the two of us again, and it'll be the way it was."

Henry's eyes studied Alec's tense face. "Maybe I oughta tell you it will be the same for you," he said, finally. "But I'm not goin' to." He ignored the startled look that came to the boy's eyes. "You've been straightforward with me, an' I aim to be the same with you," he added.

"What are you driving at, Henry?" Alec's words came fast.

"Something I been thinking about for a long time now, Alec. Something I got from just watchin' you the last six months . . . that, and what you just said. An' I want you to listen to what I have to say without flyin' off the handle. I want you to think this out with me and see if maybe I'm not right about what's botherin' you most of all."

Alec started to say something, changed his mind, and waited for Henry to continue.

"When you talk about getting it back the way it was," Henry began, choosing his words carefully, "I don't really believe it's Satan you're thinking about at all. I think it's the Black."

He waited for the outburst from Alec he thought would

come. But the boy was silent, so Henry went on, "And Satan or no other horse in the world is goin' to give you what you had with him, Alec. You might as well accept that now, before you go through life waiting for somethin' to take you back the way it was . . . somethin' that's never goin' to happen."

Napoleon nuzzled Henry's coat sleeve, pulling it. But the man's eyes never left Alec as he continued, his voice softer now: "I'm not meanin' to beat you down. I'm only tryin' to make you realize that what happened between you an' the Black comes only once in a lifetime, if at all. He was no ordinary horse, Alec. . . . He was wild and never clear broke. Yet, for some reason that's buried within that untamed heart of his, he took to you.

"Then let's take a look at what you had," Henry added hurriedly. "Here you were, just a kid, with a wild stallion only you could handle. Your love was bein' returned by an animal who had love for no one else. The Black was yours, Alec . . . as much yours as anything could possibly be. Anybody in your shoes would have felt the same way you did. It set you on top of the world."

"And it spoiled me for anything else. Is that what you mean, Henry?" Alec's lips were drawn in a tight smile. "Even for Satan?"

"Maybe I do mean that," Henry returned. "It pretty much depends on how you're goin' to look at things from now on." He paused, shifting uneasily on his feet. "I think you oughta take stock of what you got right now an' the future that's lined up for you an' Satan. He's goin' places an' you're goin' along with him. But he's no one-man horse, Alec, an' you got no right to expect him to be. Satan can be handled by 'most anybody. He's been trained to do what's expected of him. It's the way it should be . . . the only way. And he's a better horse for it . . . better than the Black, I mean. He's got the Black's speed yet he's controllable, an' that's what makes him the champion he is."

Taking Alec by the arm, he said, "C'mon down to the tack room a minute." And, as they walked along, Henry added, "Y'got to realize, too, that Satan is giving you somethin' the Black couldn't give you. The Black never could be raced. . . . He was never meant to set foot on a track with other horses. He ran wild with you in that Chicago match race; you know that as well as I do. He's no campaigner like Satan, for you'd never know what he might do from one race to another. He's as apt to fight as run."

They were at the door of the tack room when Henry stopped and turned to Alec. "And don't you think for one moment Abu Ishak doesn't know that, Alec. That's why he didn't send the Black over here to race as he said he was goin' to do, when we saw him last fall at the running of the Hopeful. Abu went back to Arabia and thought it over. An' when he did, he knew darn well it just couldn't be done. I'll bet that's why he hasn't even answered your letters."

Henry walked into the tack room, his hand on the boy's arm. He came to a halt before the picture of the Black. "What I'd do, if I were you, Alec, would be to put this picture away an' the Black along with it. I'd say to myself, 'It was good, but now it's over. It's all part of the past. . . . It's done, finished.' " Henry shrugged his shoulders. "Well, that's what I wanted to say. You know better'n me whether I been talkin' through my hat or not. You got to decide for yourself now."

Henry left Alec alone in the room.

For many minutes Alec looked steadily at the picture without moving; then, finally, he walked forward, lifting it from the wall. He carried it to the old chest and wrapped it carefully in a blanket before putting it inside and closing the lid; then he turned and walked away.

Henry was waiting for him outside the door.

"You were right, Henry," he said in a low voice. "I've been thinking of him all along . . . wishing it could be the same with Satan as it was with him. I've put him away. It's over, as you say."

Henry placed his arm across Alec's shoulders as they walked past the stalls. "We'll go out to the track early tomorrow," he said. "We won't work Satan, but we'll just hang around with him."

"When's the next race, Henry?"

"Not for a month, when we take him to Chicago. He'll be running against older horses at Arlington Park, but I don't think he'll have any trouble if he goes as he did today."

"He will," Alec said. "He couldn't run any other way."

They had reached the barn door, and Henry had switched off the lights, when they heard footsteps coming up the driveway. Alec was the first to make out his father's lanky figure in the darkness. "It's Dad," he told Henry, and the man turned on the lights again.

Seeing Alec, Mr. Ramsay said, "I've been waiting, Alec, but you were gone so long I thought I'd better bring . . ." He stopped as Henry appeared in the doorway behind Alec. "Oh, I didn't know Henry was here with you."

They stepped back into the barn as Mr. Ramsay entered, and their eyes were on the letter he held in his hand. "It's

from Arabia," he was saying. "It was in the mailbox when
we got home."

"From Abu Ishak?" Henry asked quickly, as Mr. Ramsay
handed the letter to Alec.

Shaking his head, Mr. Ramsay said, "It seems to be from
Tabari Ishak . . . at least that's the name on the return
address."

"His daughter," Henry said, turning to Alec.

The boy was holding the envelope without opening it.

"She could have addressed it for him," Henry offered. His
eyes remained on Alec's face as the boy opened the envelope
and withdrew the letter. Just as he'd told Alec, Henry didn't
think that Abu Ishak would send the Black here to race. But
he could be wrong. And, if the Black came, it would change
a lot of things . . . for him and for Alec; maybe even for
Satan. So Henry watched with anxious eyes while Alec read.

He saw the ashen white rise, beating every bit of color
from the boy's face. He saw the flood of tears come swiftly
and flow unchecked. He saw Alec's eyes close and his fingers
crush the letter within his hand.

It was Mr. Ramsay who took the letter from Alec and
straightened it out for Henry to read with him.

Arabia
June 2nd

Dear Alec,

*My father died three months ago, and we have been in
mourning. It is only now that I can write to tell you that
his death was the result of injuries suffered when he was
thrown by the stallion you know as the Black.*

Among my father's possessions was a letter to be opened

only in the event of his death. In this letter he has written that the Black is to be given to you.

It is ironical—is it not?—that my father should bequeath to you the devil responsible for his death. But for that, we would have destroyed him.

I have made arrangements with Trans-World Airlines for him to be flown to you. He will arrive in Newark, New Jersey, on the night of June the twentieth. All necessary papers, including transfer of ownership, are being sent under separate cover.

May the great Allah be with you and keep you from the same fate which befell my father.

Tabari

The Black

4

It was more than a week since Alec had received Tabari's letter, and he and Henry were sitting in the cab of their horse van, parked just off the field of the air cargo terminal in Newark, awaiting the Black.

Henry ran his hands over the steering wheel, then turned from Alec to the airport's beacon light as it cut a wide arc through the night sky. A plane went down the runway, its engines rising to a high and thunderous pitch as it took off.

"I guess I was wrong about the Black bein' a part of your past, Alec," he said. "Wrong, all right."

Alec said nothing.

"But what I said about his not bein' meant to set foot on a track still goes," Henry added, turning to the boy.

"I don't intend to race him," Alec said.

"You'll still have to watch yourself with him. I'm rememberin' y'never had much trouble. But you've been away from him a long time. Things might have changed between you an' him."

"He'll know me, Henry."

"He knew Abu, too," the man replied quietly.

A plane circled and came in. Eagerly they watched it until they saw that it was a passenger plane; then Henry glanced at his watch. "It's near midnight," he said. "Should be in any minute now." Removing his hands from the steering wheel, he noticed that they were wet with perspiration, and he wiped them a little self-consciously on the sides of his pants legs.

Alec's gaze turned to the sky; he was watching for the blinking lights of the plane, listening for the far-off drone of its engines, and all the while thinking: The Black is mine again . . . this time for keeps!

But at the cost of Abu Ishak's life.

Alec closed his eyes, shutting out the darkened sky. He had told himself over and over again that Abu was an old man. A hard fall from *any* horse could have resulted in his death. It need not have been the Black. Tabari had given him none of the details. Abu could have struck his head when he fell; any number of things could have happened. Abu's fall might even have been due to his own negligence. Perhaps the Black had stumbled while in full gallop; perhaps Abu hadn't been ready for it.

But, then, why had Tabari planned to destroy the Black, if her father's death had been accidental? Why?

The Black knew no master. Had Abu forgotten? Had he sought to dominate the fiery will of the stallion? Had he fought him and lost? Was that the reason Tabari would have the Black destroyed?

Alec opened his eyes. He didn't want to know the answers. It was much better that he never know.

I must only remember, he thought, that the Black's unlike any other horse in the world. If I remember that, I have nothing to fear. I can't dominate his will, any more than Abu could do it. I must ask of him, never demand. He must do it of his own accord, because he wants to do what I ask of him. It's not the way it should be, but it's his way. No one could change him now. . . .

They heard the drone of the plane before they were able to distinguish its light from the stars. They watched it come in, dropping lower and lower toward the field.

"This could be it," Henry said.

As the plane's wheels touched the runway, Alec made out the company's name, Trans-World, on its side. "This is it, Henry! He's here!"

They left the van and went to the wire fence which kept them from the field. The plane came off the main runway and taxied toward them, its silver body glistening in the lights that played upon it.

Henry stopped staring at the plane and looked around. Luckily, they were far from the center of the field's activity and there was no one in their immediate vicinity except for a few Trans-World cargo employees who were awaiting the plane. "Now the less fuss we have around here the better," he told Alec. "I'll check the office again to make sure all the papers are in order." Henry walked toward the lighted building to their rear, but Alec never turned from the plane.

It was a few minutes before it came to a stop a short distance from him. He saw three men in white coveralls go to meet it. The engines were raced to a high pitch by the pilot, then cut.

Alec waited for the wide cargo doors to open, his heart pounding. He turned to the gate, a little way beyond him, and to the man attending it; then his gaze swept to the Trans-World office as he looked anxiously for Henry.

Turning back to the plane, he found the doors still unopened. He was moving along the fence toward the gateman when Henry came running up to him.

"We can take him once he's off," Henry said. "No quarantine is necessary. He's been checked out."

"Let's get up to the gate then," Alec replied, without stopping.

"Take it easy," his friend cautioned. "They'll get him off all right. It's just a consignment to them now, so let's not make it any more than that."

Reaching the gateman, Henry handed him the clearance he'd received from the office, and the man checked it against his list. "They'll have him off in a few minutes," he said.

Alec saw the cargo doors open. A man appeared and called to the men on the ground. He left the doorway, but reappeared a few seconds later, pushing out a long wooden ramp. When they had the ramp set up it extended from the doors of the plane to the ground.

Suddenly the long, piercing whistle of the Black shattered the night, but died quickly beneath the roar of a plane going down the runway.

Alec's hand went quickly to the chain extending across the entrance to the field; then he stopped, turning to Henry. "Maybe I could help them," he said.

Henry smiled at the gateman, "We're a little anxious about our horse."

"No need to worry," the gateman replied. "We sort of specialize in carrying horses and animals of all kinds. Never had any trouble yet."

Henry nodded agreeably, but Alec turned anxiously back to the plane. The Black uttered another shrill scream; then came the sharp ring of his hoofs striking metal.

"Some are a little harder to handle than others," the gateman was saying. "But it's all in knowing how. That fellow inside the plane is a professional animal handler. He rides along with every animal we carry. Just another of the services our company provides its clients."

"As y'say," Henry agreed, smiling. "It's all in knowin' how."

"Yeah, that and having the equipment," the gateman added. "We can make our planes into regular flying stables, when necessary. We use collapsible stalls with a soft rubber matting and wooden shavings for the horses to stand on. Everything for their comfort, you might say. But if they give us any trouble, this fellow can take care of them; he's got a firm hand." He turned to the plane. "Yours is the only animal we're carrying tonight. The rest is freight. He should have had him out by now. It usually doesn't take . . ." He stopped abruptly, his eyes on the doorway.

The Black stood just within the plane, the animal handler at his head.

"There he is now," the gateman said. "We'll have him off right away."

"Sure," Henry said uneasily, for he could see the man was having trouble. He put his hand on Alec's arm.

The Black shook his head savagely as the man jerked hard on the lead shank he held short in his hand. The stallion snorted in contempt and his eyes blazed defiantly; then he moved out of the doorway and onto the ramp. For a moment he remained still, his eyelids blinking in the glare of the floodlights and his ears pricked to the sound of an incoming plane.

He was like a giant statue. Arrogant and noble, he stood there; his small head, crowned by silky foretop, was set majestically on his long and highly arched neck, and no sculptor could have done justice to the suppleness and fineness of line of his beautifully molded body.

The man at his head jerked again on the lead shank, trying to move him down the ramp. Tall and long-limbed, the stallion took two steps; then, without warning, he reared, carrying the man with him.

No longer was he beautiful to behold, but a ranting, raging beast, fighting for his freedom! To bring him down, the man struck him hard across the muzzle. The Black swelled to greater fury at the impact of the blow, and, when his forefeet touched the ramp, he bolted forward.

Alec was running to him when the Black pulled himself free of the man's desperate grip on his halter. Jumping clear of the ramp, the stallion broke into a gallop. He started toward the runway, but stopped before the outburst of a plane's engines. Whirling, he came back, his eyes white and starting from his head. He swerved when he came upon Alec, and swept by, perilously close to the boy.

His whirlwind charge came to a sudden stop. He shook his disheveled head, and his nostrils filled out. Turning again, he faced Alec. His large eyes were upon the boy, his ears cupped to the sound of Alec's voice. He jerked his head upward and held it still, his every sense keyed to the utmost.

"Black, Black," Alec kept repeating, while his eyes held those of the stallion. He saw every sign of impending recognition, but he could only wait and hope.

Now the Black was tense and rigid, with only his nostrils quivering. For many minutes he seemed undecided. His flashing eyes left Alec to move back and forth, slowly, as his head turned. He moved neither toward Alec nor away from him. He stood alert and confident in his strength.

Alec kept talking, caring little what he said. It was only the sound of his voice that mattered. His voice and scent were what the Black remembered.

The stallion turned to him again, listening intently, smelling with long, delicate nostrils; then he came forward, trotting with high head and tail.

Alec reached out to him, and the stallion did not move away at his touch. The boy's arms swept around him and he buried his head in the long mane.

He heard Henry's voice, but he did not turn to him.

"Take him out, while you got him," Henry was saying excitedly. "Let's get outa here before . . ."

The Black moved nervously at the sound of Henry's voice. Alec took him by the halter. "Come on, fellow. We're going home."

After a moment's hesitation, the Black moved with him. Henry had led the men away from the gate, but their gaze followed Alec as he took the stallion from the field.

Alec led the Black toward the van, Henry walking a little behind them.

"Nice and quiet just like he wanted," Henry muttered to

himself. "I shoulda known better than to expect it. But it could have been worse. If he'd gotten away, everyone on the field would have known it, an' it'd be in the papers tomorrow. As it is, these Trans-World guys are just glad to get rid of him."

Henry's gaze swept over the Black as the stallion walked nimbly beside the boy. He was quiet now; there was none of the savagery displayed only a few minutes before. Nor was he fidgeting or capering nervously; only his head moved, and he turned it back and forth, observing everything about him. Yet he was a picture of pure blood and fiery energy, ready to burst into action at the slightest impulse.

Henry stopped in his tracks, for Alec had the stallion at the van and he was shying away from the ramp. Henry started forward; then, thinking better of it, stopped again and stayed behind.

Alec waited patiently for his horse, talking to him all the while. He turned him around in a circle several times, then led him to the ramp again and stepped upon it. The Black hesitated, then followed, his hoofs resounding on the wooden boards.

Running to the van, Henry pushed the ramp inside. He was closing the door when Alec called, "I'll ride back here with him."

"As if I didn't know," Henry said.

It was well over an hour later when Henry drove up to the barn in Flushing. He backed the van to a grassy knoll just to the side of the driveway, got out and opened the door. Alec pushed the ramp over to him and Henry set one end down on the knoll. The descent from the van was gradual, and Henry knew Alec wouldn't have any trouble getting the stallion down. He went to the barn, opened the doors wide and switched on the lights. Napoleon raised his head, neighing softly.

"You've an old friend comin' to see you," Henry told him. "Maybe you'll recognize him."

Henry turned from the door at the sound of the Black coming down the ramp. Alec had him off and was leading him toward the barn. The stallion's lips, eyes and ears were all in motion.

"He knows where he is, Henry," Alec called. "Just look at him!"

As the Black entered the barn, his ears pricked forward at sight of Napoleon. He neighed shrilly and moved quickly across the floor. Napoleon stretched out his head to him, while the Black moved close, his nostrils quivering.

"Better be careful with him," Henry warned both Alec and Napoleon.

But Napoleon had no fear of the Black, and he shoved his gray head hard against the stallion. The Black stood still, watching him curiously.

After a few minutes Alec opened the door to the empty stall. The Black turned to it, his long nostrils quivering; then, without a word from the boy, he went inside.

Henry waited while Alec fed and watered the Black, but when he saw that the boy meant to stay inside the stall he walked slowly toward the barn door.

This is the way Alec wanted it, all right, he thought. Just the Black and him all over again. But it can't go on. No more than it could with Satan. Someone's going to learn about the Black's being here, and when the news breaks the Lord only knows where it'll end. But no need to tell him that. Not now. Let him have it the way he wants for as long as he can. It'll be short enough. . . . It can't last, not with a horse like the Black.

Quietly Henry opened the door and stepped out into the night, leaving Alec alone with his horse.

Riding High!

5

It was very early the next morning when Alec returned to the barn after only a few hours' sleep. He went directly to the Black, running his hand through the stallion's long mane to remove the straw that had matted the hair.

"You were down last night," he said softly.

The Black nickered, following him to the water pail that hung in a corner. Alec removed the pail from its bracket and left the stall, closing the door behind him; then he went into Napoleon's stall and got his pail, too, before going to the water faucet outside the barn. Returning, he first went to Napoleon, setting his pail up for him; then he entered the stallion's stall again. Instead of placing the pail in the corner, he held it while the Black pushed his small, finely drawn muzzle down to the water. Alec's fingers touched the mole-soft skin as the stallion drank.

A few minutes later Alec was at the feedbox, scooping up

containers of oats for the Black and Napoleon. And, while the stallion ate, he cleaned the stall and pitched in some fresh straw, bedding it down well; then he went quickly to the chest in the tack room. He took out the brushes and currycomb, and was about to close the lid when he saw the folded blanket. He picked it up carefully, his eyes turning to the far wall of the room; then he unwrapped the blanket from about the Black's picture and hung it once more in its proper place on the wall. His eyes shining, he turned from it and left the room.

The Black moved uneasily as Alec brought the brush across his body, but the boy moved with him, unmindful of the fiery brightness coming into the stallion's eyes. Alec went to the rear of the stallion, brushing out the straw from his tail; then he stooped to pick up the Black's feet, going from one to the other, cleaning them of the dirt and manure that was packed within the hoofs. It was only when he straightened, close to the Black's head, that he saw the unusual light in the stallion's eyes. Aware of the fury that smoldered within the Black, he stepped closer to him and raised the brush to the stallion's lips.

"It's nothing to be afraid of," he said, as the Black nuzzled the brush. "It can't hurt you. And you're not worried about me. I'm supposed to be here . . . no place else."

Taking a cloth from his pocket, Alec ran it along the stallion's neck; then he turned away from him, going over the sleek body and down the long, sinewy legs. When he straightened, he found the Black licking his feedbox clean of the last remaining oats. The stallion's eyes were soft and dark again, and Alec knew that any uncertainty the Black might have had regarding his right to handle him was gone.

To the rear of the stall was a sliding door, and it was to this that Alec now went. His hand was on it when the Black came to him. The stallion's small ears were pitched forward, his head craned high. Sliding the door open, Alec stepped to one side.

For a few seconds the Black remained rigidly still in the daylight that came through the doorway; his lips shriveled and he snorted through dilated nostrils. Cautiously he stepped outside, his eyes in constant motion, his ears pricked and keyed to pick up the slightest sound.

A narrow runway led behind the barn to the field. The Black turned to the green grass, neighing for joy at sight of it; then he was moving at a slow trot, his long tail streaming behind him.

Leaving the door open, Alec ran back through the barn and outside. He went on to the high rail fence, and his eyes were on the stallion as the Black swept from the runway into the field. He watched him change from a trot into a slow canter.

Alec climbed to the top rail of the fence and sat there, content in the knowledge that nothing in the world could equal what he had again for his very own.

The stallion cantered alongside the stone wall, but stopped when he came to the hollow at the far end. He stood still for a moment, then trotted along the rim of the hollow and across the field. Reaching the stone fence on the opposite side, he stopped to look through the trees toward the boulevard. A car went down the street, its engine whining loudly in the early-morning stillness. The Black snorted and came up the field. Reaching the fence at Alec's end, he turned with it. He stopped a short distance from the boy, his

slender neck arched sharply at the crest, his head cocked a
little to one side.

One moment he was still, but the next he had broken out
into furious action! With a snort he bolted, flinging his
hindlegs and quarters high in the air. He ran a few yards,
then his hindlegs thrashed the air again. Without stopping,
he burst into a fast gallop and quickly reached the end of the
field. He stopped there and lowered himself to the ground.
Rolling over on his back, he shoved his body into the soft
earth, grunting with pleasure as his legs moved above him.
He was up quickly, once more bursting into full gallop and
slowing only when he came to the stone fence; then he
turned with amazing swiftness and came up the field again.
This time he ran to Alec and stopped before him.

The boy's hand reached out to touch the disheveled head,
to run down the satin neck. The Black was close to him, so
close that it was a simple matter to slip lightly from the
fence onto the stallion's back. He was on him before he
knew it. . . . It had come instinctively, naturally, as though
each had known it was the way it should be.

The stallion moved forward, without bolting, and his gait
was effortless and easy to ride. How different he was from
Satan, Alec thought. For only when the Black's burly son
was in full gallop was he easy to ride; only then did Satan
lose the ponderousness that was so much in evidence at any
other gait.

The Black broke into a gallop and Alec slid forward,
pressing his hands close to the sides of the stallion's neck. He
had forgotten, too, how high the Black carried his head even
in full gallop. Satan always pushed his head forward and his
ears would lie back, flat and heavy against his head. The two

horses were so different in many ways, yet beneath Alec's knees worked the same giant muscles that helped provide each horse with his tremendous power and speed.

The Black's strides swallowed the ground and he swerved abruptly to avoid the hollow. Alec moved with him, glorying in the strength of the stallion as he leveled out again and went back up the field.

Half-asleep, Henry heard the rhythmic beat of running hoofs. He turned uneasily in his bed, his back to the open window that looked out upon the field. His eyes remained closed as he mumbled, "I'm hearing things. It's Sunday. I don't have to go to the track today. Satan is taking a rest. No horse within miles . . . only Napoleon, and he's not working today, either. Must be early . . . very early."

He opened his eyes to look at the clock on his bureau. It was only a little past six o'clock. He was closing his eyes when the pounding beat of hoofs came again. He sat straight up in bed. The Black! Alec!

He ran to the window, carrying his bed covers with him in his haste. He saw the fast-moving black figure coming up the field. But he didn't see Alec, for the boy was stuck like a burr high on the Black's withers and half-hidden by the whipping mane. Henry glanced at the barn, then back at the running stallion before he saw the boy.

"That crazy kid!" he said. "He shoulda waited for me."

Henry reached for his clothes on a nearby chair and pulled them on hurriedly, but his eyes never left Alec and the racing Black.

The stallion's strides shortened as he neared the fence, slowing to turn across the field. Henry saw then that he wore neither bridle nor saddle, and that Alec was guiding him by pressing his hands hard against the Black's neck.

"Alec can't see anythin' bad in that horse," Henry said, shaking his head. "He never will, an' maybe that's why he gets away with it." Henry drew on his shirt more slowly. "No sense in my gettin' excited now. He's up and havin' no trouble."

Henry marveled at the Black's bursts of speed in the short field. There was a wildness to his every move, yet it seemed the stallion was ready to obey Alec's slightest command. Now the great strides slowed as Alec moved his body back and away from the long neck. Henry saw the Black paw the air at a bird which rose a few feet in front of him, but he did it without breaking stride.

A short distance from the hollow Alec brought him to a stop, and the stallion lowered his head to graze.

Henry turned away from the window, looking for his shoes. When he found them, he sat down.

"If I could only keep it this way for him," he said aloud. "If it was just him and the Black, I don't think he'd have trouble with him. But just let the press get wise he's here and they'll raise such a clamor Alec will have to race him. It'll be a different story then. . . . Put that devil on a track with the wind of other stallions in his nostrils an' he'll forget all about Alec's bein' up there on his back. I don't want to see that. I aim to do all I can to keep it from happenin'."

Henry bent down, and long after he had his shoes on he remained hunched over, his eyes focused on the floor. When he straightened, his face was a brilliant red from the blood that had rushed to his head. But tiny flecks of light pinpointed his eyes as he said excitedly, "I've got it. I think I have the answer." He rushed from the room.

Alec and the Black were still at the far end of the field when Henry reached the fence. He called, but the boy didn't hear him. Henry turned away from the field at the creaking of the iron gate and saw Mr. Ramsay walking hurriedly up the driveway. It was obvious that Alec's father had dressed as hastily as Henry, for his shirt was unbuttoned, his hair was uncombed and he wore slippers instead of shoes.

When Mr. Ramsay reached him, Henry saw the concern in the man's eyes. "Alec's all right," he said assuredly.

"I suppose he is." Mr. Ramsay's gaze remained on Alec and the Black for some time before he turned to Henry. "He's certainly not having any trouble with him," he added. "But what do you think, Henry? How dangerous is the Black?"

Henry avoided Mr. Ramsay's eyes. "You got to have respect for what any horse might do," he said. "An' Alec has plenty of respect for the Black."

"I know that, Henry," Mr. Ramsay paused. "Then you don't think Alec will have any trouble with him?"

Henry turned to him. "There are some things you can't explain," he replied slowly. "The Black's willingness to do what Alec wants him to do is one of 'em. Under normal circumstances I think Alec will always be able to control him."

" 'Under normal circumstances'," Mr. Ramsay repeated. "What do you mean by that, Henry?"

Nodding his head toward Alec and the Black, Henry said, "The two of 'em alone just like they are now."

"But that's the way it's going to be," Mr. Ramsay returned quickly.

"Not if people find out the Black's here," Henry said. "They'll have Alec racin' him before he knows it. All the kid is thinkin' about now is to keep the Black for himself, but once the press start building up interest in a race between the Black and some of the other champs, especially Satan, he'll race him just to find out for himself which is the fastest horse. It's in him to find out one way or another, and if a race is more or less forced on him, he'll go through with it."

"And you don't think the Black should race. Is that it, Henry?"

"I know he'd cause a lot of trouble on a track, what with all the excitement and other stallions around. An' I doubt that his love for Alec would be strong enough to overcome his natural instinct to fight. I may be wrong . . . but I'd sooner not find out by watching it."

"I suppose you're right, Henry," Mr. Ramsay said gravely. "But there's a chance no one will know he's here."

"You can't keep a horse like the Black where everyone can see him without somebody gettin' wise," Henry returned quickly. "But I got an idea, Mr. Ramsay. You know that farm upstate that Alec and I had in mind to buy when Satan was through racin'?"

Nodding, Mr. Ramsay said, "You two were going to start your own stud farm."

"Well, now we don't have to wait for Satan," Henry said. "We got the Black. An' I'm goin' to suggest to Alec we buy that farm right now an' take the Black there."

"Henry! That's a great idea!" Mr. Ramsay half-shouted. "We've got the money for it. He'll do it. I'm sure he will."

Together they turned to the field, and Henry was about to call Alec when he saw a tractor-trailer coming down the boulevard. He decided to wait until it had passed before attracting Alec's attention. Suddenly there was a sharp, shattering retort from the truck as it backfired. The Black bolted.

Alec lurched backward as the stallion's swift move caught him unprepared. The boy's hands reached behind him to find the Black's quarters, then his right leg swung over the stallion and he slid off the Black, his feet landing lightly on the ground.

The Black slowed to a trot when he neared the fence and saw the two men standing on the other side. Snorting, he shook his head, then turned in Alec's direction. For a few minutes he looked at the boy walking up the field, then he lowered his head to graze again.

When Alec neared them Henry said, "You weren't ready for him. That's the way you get hurt."

Alec stopped beside the stallion, his hand upon him; then he went over to the fence. "I know," he said. "It won't happen again."

"There's too much noise around here for him, Alec," his father said.

"Yeah," Henry agreed quickly. "Not enough room, either. Why don't you take him outa here?"

The boy turned from his father to Henry, his eyes puzzled. "Take him where?"

"Your father and I were just talkin' about that farm we were goin' to buy, where we could breed and raise our own colts. I'm ready to start right now, Alec. We got more than enough money with what Satan has won."

"And I'm ready too," Mr. Ramsay added hastily. "That is . . . if you'll hire me as your accountant."

Bewildered, Alec turned from them to the Black, then back to Henry. "You mean with the Black?"

"Why not? We've got our stallion. We don't have to wait for Satan."

Alec's face was brilliant with eagerness, but then his eyes

clouded as he asked, "But what about you, Henry? You couldn't come now . . . not with Satan racing."

"No, I couldn't," Henry admitted. "But that's not stoppin' you from goin' ahead and setting things up for us. Get the farm in working order an' even start thinkin' about the mares we oughta buy to breed to the Black. You'll have plenty to do, Alec."

"And I'll help you," his father said.

Henry saw the doubt in Alec's eyes and he added hurriedly, "Meanwhile, I'll be moving along with Satan this summer. My business is training horses, Alec. You belong at the other end of this partnership deal. You'll be top man in raising our colts and fillies, teaching 'em to get along with people and"—Henry smiled—"making it easy for me like you did with Satan."

"But it wouldn't be the same without you around, Henry."

"I'll be around, Alec, an' don't you think I won't be. I expect to set up a training track in that upper pasture an' we can work the horses there."

"If it could only be that way," Alec said eagerly.

"No reason why it can't. Not if we go at it the right way by buying the farm now, like I said, and working toward it."

"But," Alec asked, "if we do this, Henry, and I stay at the farm with the Black, who will ride Satan?"

"A lot of good jocks would give anything to be up on him. Lenny Sansone worked him all winter and spring, so I guess he'd be the one." Henry paused. "But you could get away from the farm to ride him in his races just like you've been doin', unless . . ."

"I want to make a clean break," Alec finished for him. "Is that what you mean, Henry?"

The man nodded. "It's up to you, Alec," he said. "No reason why you can't do both."

The Black cropped the grass close beside Alec and the boy put his hand on him. "I'll stay with him, Henry," he said slowly. "I do belong at the other end. . . ."

Satan Wears His Crown

6

Four weeks later, Alec sat close to his bedroom radio, awaiting the results of the Arlington Handicap being raced in Chicago. Satan was running and any moment the race would be over, and the results announcing the winner would come.

He turned to the open window through which he could see the Black grazing in shadows cast by the late afternoon sun. He was glad that he had made the swift, clean break from the track. He belonged with the Black, and now they'd be together always.

Yet this was not the end, but rather the beginning . . . the beginning of everything for both of them. No longer was he a jockey. He had become a breeder of horses. And for his stallion he had the Black, the fastest horse in the world! In two weeks' time they'd be at the new farm. Hopeful Farm he had decided to call it, for they were going there with great hopes for the future. He would be the breeder and have charge of the raising and breaking of the colts; Henry would be the trainer, and Dad, the business manager.

Why shouldn't they make a go of it? Weren't Satan's great triumphs on the track positive proof that the Black could pass on his speed to his get? And what better way could they spend Satan's winnings than by investing the money in this farm, where other sons and daughters of the Black would be bred and raised? Even now, he could see the foals running close beside their mothers, timid and a little afraid; while in another pasture would stand the Black, watching them and knowing they were his.

None of them would ever take the Black's place, no more than Satan had done. But they would have *his* blood, and they would go forth to the track, sounding the name of their great sire, to establish forever the stamina and speed of the Black.

Unable to sit still at the prospect of what lay ahead, Alec rose from his chair and went to the window. He stood there, watching the Black. Just a few more weeks to go, he told the stallion, then you'll have acres and acres of pasture over which to run as far and as fast as you like. *Just two more weeks!*

His thoughts turned to Henry, as he remembered how disappointed his friend had been when they learned that they couldn't have possession of the farm until the middle of August. Henry had wanted to see the Black and Alec at the farm before he left with Satan for Chicago. But a few weeks' delay wasn't very long to wait for something they meant to share the rest of their lives. And that's what Alec had told Henry before the trainer had taken his reluctant but necessary departure.

Alec turned quickly away from the window as the sports commentator said, "Adding another gem to an already brilliant crown, Satan slammed down the stretch to win the rich Arlington Handicap by ten lengths over Star Pilot in the new world's record time of one minute fifty-eight seconds for the mile and a quarter!"

Alec let out a yell, but cut it short as the commentator went on.

"The burly three-year-old champion clearly established his greatness by decisively beating older horses whom he had not met before today. Lenny Sansone, piloting Satan, displayed a sparkling bit of riding by getting his mount out of a tight pocket coming into the homestretch and bringing Satan on to pass Star Pilot, last year's Kentucky Derby winner, in the run for the wire. Stepson, the West Coast champion, came in third, followed by . . ."

When the commentator had finished, Alec switched off the radio, turning again to the window. His eyes were bright as he said aloud, "One minute fifty-eight seconds for the mile and a quarter!" He shook his head in amazement. Never had he dreamed any horse, even the Black, was capable of running so fast!

In the field, the Black left his grazing to move quickly toward the barn. Alec watched his long, effortless strides. "I wonder," he thought aloud, "if Satan could beat him, too?" He paused, his gaze following the stallion until he came to a stop at the barn fence. "No," Alec said finally. "Satan couldn't do it. No horse could."

With his head craned high over the fence, the Black whistled. His call was echoed by a shrill neigh from the street, and Alec saw Napoleon coming along at a shuffling trot.

Tony sat high in the wagon seat, the long reins held lightly in his big hands.

Alec called to him, and Tony waved back. The boy went downstairs and outside, where he ran across the street to open the iron gate for Tony.

The huckster's black eyes were bright as he said, "See, Aleec, I no need to cluck to my Nappy when he sees the Black; then he just go like the wind all by himself!"

Napoleon went up the driveway, Alec running beside the wagon, which was now empty of its daily cargo of fresh fruits and vegetables. Tony was the last of his kind in Flushing.

"Satan just won that Chicago race, Tony!" Alec shouted. "And he set a new world record!"

Nodding his heavy head, Tony said, "So I am not one bit surprised, Aleec. I expect him to win all the time."

When they reached the barn, Tony left his seat to unharness Napoleon, while Alec went for a pail of water. The old gray moved about impatiently, and Tony said, "You stand-a still, Napoleon. You think you're one young colt again!"

Alec returned, lifting the water pail to Napoleon's muzzle. "But Satan beat older horses today, Tony . . . and they were the very best in the country!"

Shrugging his shoulders, Tony said, "Satan, he's-a young horse and very strong. So why should he not beat older horses, Aleec? It's-a youth that makes him win." Tony's hand swept down Napoleon's neck as he added, "You take Nappy, for example. When he was-a young, he like to run all the time. But now maybe just once in a long time he feel like it. Or you take the Black." They turned to the stallion, who was moving uneasily up and down alongside the fence.

"He no have the speed he had few years ago, I bet. Satan could beat him now, too."

"I don't think so," Alec replied quickly. "The Black is still young, Tony. He's as fast as he ever was, and maybe even faster."

"So you think, Aleec. But I no think so. It's being young that gives the speed." Tony turned from the Black, and, slipping the halter on Napoleon, said, "Now I put him in the field."

Alec went to the field gate and slipped through the rails. Coming to him, the Black nuzzled his shirt and Alec pressed his head close to the stallion. "Imagine anyone thinking you're an old man at seven," he said softly. "There's no horse in the world who could keep up with you . . . even Satan. He did a mile and a quarter in one fifty-eight today, Black. But you could run faster than that, couldn't you?"

The stallion's head turned to Napoleon as Tony led the gray gelding toward the gate. Giving the Black a carrot, Alec took him a short distance down the field and held him until Tony had Napoleon in the field.

The old gray didn't go to the Black, but moved past him, going down the field at a slow gallop. For a moment the stallion watched Napoleon; then suddenly he snorted and bolted after the gray.

Alec helped Tony close the gate before turning once again to the horses. The Black was playfully circling Napoleon as the gray continued his slow gallop. But finally Napoleon came to a stop and lowered his head to graze. The Black halted, too, inquisitively watching him. He waited for a short time with only his eyes moving; then he was off again, charging back and forth before the gray. Napoleon went on with his grazing, seemingly unmindful of the Black's furious action. But when the stallion lowered himself to the ground and rolled over on his back, Napoleon raised his head to watch; then he too carefully got down and pushed his back into the soft earth.

"Nappy no fear him," Tony said proudly, as they watched the thrashing legs.

"No reason why he should," Alec returned. "The Black is his best friend and he knows it." Pausing, the boy added, "If you want to go home, Tony, I'll bring in Napoleon when it gets dark."

"Okay, Aleec," Tony said, moving away from the fence. "I think I go then. It's-a been one hard day."

Long after Tony had gone, Alec remained beside the fence, watching his horse. Until today he had felt confident that no horse in the world could match the Black's speed. But Satan's new world record for the mile and a quarter had changed things. Now he wasn't sure. And he knew he wanted to be sure before he took the Black to the farm.

There was an easy way to find out, and Alec decided to try it . . . the next morning, at dawn, in the park.

Alec had his clock beneath his pillow, so when the alarm went off at four o'clock the following morning he alone heard its muffled ring. Hurriedly he reached for it and silenced the alarm. He lay there for a moment, listening to the incessant chant of the katydids in the field. But there was no sound of rain, and only this could have postponed his plans. Silently he got out of bed and pulled on his jeans and sweat shirt. He sat down to put on his socks and boots, all the while listening to the snoring of his parents, who slept in the next room. When he rose from the chair, he went quickly across the darkened room to the desk near the window; there he found his baseball cap and pulled it snugly about his head. Opening the top drawer of the desk, he removed a silver-cased stopwatch and wound it before carefully placing it in his pocket.

One minute and fifty-eight seconds for the mile and a quarter. The Black was going out to beat Satan's record!

With the watch ticking inside his pocket, Alec went down the stairs. He moved slowly, quietly, for he didn't want anyone to know what he was about to do. It would take only a short while. There would be no traffic on the back streets at this hour, and the park would be empty. He knew exactly where he would go. The stretch of bridle path from the seventh tee of the park's golf course to the towering elm tree opposite the ninth hole green was just a mile and a quarter. He and Henry had measured it accurately over a year ago, when they had jogged Satan there prior to his going to the track. But this morning the Black wouldn't be jogging. He'd be going all out, running his very fastest! It would be over and done with in a very short time. They'd be back at the barn even before Tony and Napoleon left for the market.

Leaving the house, Alec ran across the street to the iron gate. He opened it wide, and didn't shut it behind him. Reaching the barn, he went inside without turning on the lights. The Black whinnied and Alec went to him, stroking the small head for a few minutes before going on to the tack room. He returned, carrying the light racing saddle and bridle.

Alec worked quickly in the darkness. The Black moved

uneasily when the saddle pad, followed by the saddle, was put on his back. But he quieted at the touch of Alec's hands and the sound of the boy's voice. "You're going light right now," Alec said. "No feed until later."

After Alec had the bridle on him, he led the Black from the barn. The stallion's nostrils dilated and he snorted repeatedly as he moved beside Alec. The boy took him to the bench in front of the barn, and mounted from there.

His knees pressed hard against the muscled withers, Alec took the Black down the driveway. And only for a fraction of a second did he hesitate before riding him through the gate and out onto the street.

Henry wouldn't approve of what he was doing, he knew. For just before Henry had left he had cautioned him to do nothing that might arouse anyone's suspicions that it was the Black which was stabled in the barn. But Henry wouldn't know, neither would anyone else. This was something just between him and the Black.

After a few minutes Alec turned the stallion onto a narrow back street, where the shoulders were of dirt. And as the Black's hoofs struck the earth in place of the hard pavement Alec let him go into a slow canter. He'd be at the park just at dawn . . . he'd be back at the barn soon after. There was nothing to worry about. The Black was ready for a fast workout, after having spent the last few weeks running about the field. It would do him a lot of good . . . Alec's hand went to the watch within his pocket. "I'll know," he said aloud, "even if no one else does. And I want to know."

The road led directly to the park, and within fifteen minutes after leaving the barn Alec and the Black were on the bridle path. The stallion was pulling now, but the boy was able to hold him to a slow gallop. He talked to him all the while, well knowing that no bit would hold the stallion once he took it in mind to run. He was not up on Satan, he reminded himself. He must remember he had no control over the stallion other than the Black's willingness to obey him. The stallion was eager to go, his every movement showed it.

"Just a little while now," Alec told him. "Just a few minutes more, then it'll be all right." Once he gave the Black his head, there would be no stopping him until he had run himself out.

The bridle path encircled the baseball diamond, and just on the other side was the golf course and the seventh tee. It was from there he'd start.

The gray light of dawn had come. He had figured everything just about right so far. The Black shook his head, his strides became longer. Alec rose high in his short stirrups, standing almost upright in them, his weight forward of the horse's center of balance. He knew he wouldn't be able to hold the stallion in check much longer. But they were almost at the start now, and he wouldn't need to.

They had left the baseball diamond behind and were nearing the seventh tee. Far across the green fairway of the golf course Alec could see the tall elm tree that for them would be the finish of this race against time. The tree was directly opposite from where they were now, with the bridle path encircling the far edges of the fairway in the shape of a horseshoe. There was a long stretch ahead of them, a turn, then another stretch down past the tall elm.

Rising still higher in his stirrups, Alec worked hard to bring the Black under control. "No running start," he said.

"It's got to be just as it would be in a race. Easy now, fella . . . wait a minute . . . slow . . . let's walk now. That's it. Nice and easy."

They were just about opposite the seventh tee. Alec removed the stopwatch from his pocket, and his thumb was on the stem. A slight touch was all that was necessary to set the hands in motion.

"Steady," Alec said softly. "Down to a stop now. We're at the barrier. No moving forward. Stand still now, boy." He knew this would be far different from riding the Black in the field, and his excitement was transmitted to the stallion. The Black's ears pitched forward and didn't move again; his eyes were fixed straight ahead. It was very evident he knew what was coming.

Momentarily his prancing stopped and he was still. Now Alec's weight rested just off the saddle and only his knees gripped the stallion. Simultaneously he released the Black and pressed the stem of the stopwatch.

He was ready for the break. He had no doubt that the Black could get away from a standing start faster than Satan. He was expecting the swift surge forward, the great strides that would send the stallion into full gallop almost immediately.

But when it actually came he realized that even he had underestimated the speed of the Black's break. It was like being hurled from the mouth of a giant catapult! And as he pressed his head close to the Black's straining neck, his breath came short at the sheer, uncontrolled power unleashed beneath him!

The stallion raced down the bridle path, his hoofs sending the soft dirt flying behind him. Already he had leveled out and was running wild, with no thought of anything but to run as he had been born to run.

The wind tore at Alec's face and blurred his eyes so he could not see. The reins were still clenched between his hands, but he knew they were of little use to him now. Nothing could stop the stallion. Not until he had run himself out would he respond to the reins. But it didn't matter now. Nothing mattered except the watch ticking off the seconds until they reached the tall elm.

The Black bore down upon the turn, and as he swept into it, Alec's hand touched his neck and the stallion moved close to the inside. Alec heard himself clucking to the stallion, urging him on to still greater speed as they passed the halfway mark. Once again the bridle path straightened and the homestretch was ahead of them!

Alec called to the stallion, but his words were lost in the wind created by the straining body. Tremendous strides brought them down to the elm tree with lightning swiftness. There was no need to urge the Black to run faster, for he was going all out. The tall elm tree was but a hundred yards ahead . . . then fifty, ten and five! Alec's thumb pushed the stem of the watch as they swept past.

The race was over, but there was no slackening of the Black's speed. After going another quarter of a mile, Alec drew back on the reins, but still there was no response from the stallion.

A park road now ran parallel to the bridle path, but Alec knew there were no intersections for three miles and the Black would have run himself out long before then.

The stallion ran another quarter-mile before there was any noticeable shortening of stride. Alec drew back on the reins again, and gradually the Black slowed. He had the stallion almost under control when he saw a car coming down the road. The Black leveled out again at sight of it, and it wasn't until they had passed the car and left it far behind that Alec managed to bring him down to a slow gallop.

Alec's hand moved down the lathered neck. "Take it easy now," he said softly. "It's over." He settled back in the saddle as the stallion responded to his commands and went into a long, loping canter.

It was only then that Alec's gaze dropped to the watch he held in the palm of his hand. Had he any doubt that the Black had beaten Satan's record of one minute fifty-eight seconds?

"No," he answered himself. "Certainly Satan never could have run faster than the Black has just gone. I have proof of it right here in my hand."

His fingers unclenched to disclose the face of the watch. Alec looked at it with incredulous eyes.

One minute fifty-nine seconds! The Black's time was one whole second behind the record Satan had set yesterday!

He drew the watch closer to his eyes. He couldn't believe what the hands told him. Satan couldn't have run faster! No horse could!

But Satan had. The proof of it was here . . . right here in his hand.

The Black slowed to an uneasy crabstep, his head moving to the left, then to the right. Alec's hand went up and down his neck, but even as he stroked the stallion he frantically sought excuses for the Black's failure to break Satan's record.

Perhaps something was wrong with the watch.

No, it couldn't be that, he decided. He'd had it at the jeweler's for cleaning less than a month ago. It was accurate.

Then it was the bridle path. It was much too soft. It wasn't meant for speed. Satan had had a lightning-fast track . . . good and firm, the way he liked it.

Yes, there was no doubt but that the Black could have made faster time on a track. But he had to remember that the Black had had no other horses with which to contend, while Satan had. Satan had been pocketed coming into the homestretch. The radio commentator had mentioned Lenny Sansone's getting him out of it. Satan might have lowered the record still more except for that.

"Satan is in excellent condition," Alec said aloud, "while the Black hasn't been near a track. He's not in shape."

But he knew that he had realized this all along. He had expected the Black to beat Satan's record in spite of it. Now, he knew he had been wrong. In order to beat Satan, the Black would have to be properly conditioned. And, even then, it would be close . . . so very close.

But such a race would never take place. Hadn't he decided not to race the Black again? He was going to take him away to the farm.

But would it be the same now, knowing that perhaps Satan could beat the Black?

The stallion's shrill whistle aroused Alec from his thoughts. It was getting late, and he should be on his way back to the barn. Turning the Black, he saw the car coming toward them; it could be the same one they had passed a few minutes ago. Alec's face tightened as he watched it come to a stop and made out the word POLICE lettered on its side.

The door of the car opened and a policeman got out, calling him. Alec slid down from his saddle and stepped in front of the Black. He saw the summons book in the officer's hand and bit his lower lip. The stallion moved about uneasily and Alec took a few more steps in front of him as he awaited the policeman.

"And what jockey do you think you might be?" the police officer asked sarcastically when he had reached Alec.

The boy was silent.

The policeman turned back the cover of his summons book. "It's against the law to gallop a horse in a public park," he said. "You know that?"

"I didn't know," Alec said. "Really, officer, I . . ."

"You know now. Your name?"

Alec hesitated, then said, "Alexander Ramsay."

"Alexander Ramsay," the policeman repeated. "Sounds familiar. Did I ever book you before?"

"No . . . never before."

The policeman turned back to his summons book. "Address?"

Alec gave it to him, then said, "But it's so early, officer. No one is around. I couldn't have hurt anyone."

"Not the point," the police officer said curtly. "No exceptions." Handing Alec the summons, he turned to the Black. "This your horse?"

Alec nodded, moving the stallion away as the policeman stepped closer.

"What's wrong with him?"

"Nothing's wrong with him," Alec said. But his grip on the bridle tightened when he saw the brightness of the stallion's eyes. "If that's all, I'll be going now," he added quickly.

But the policeman had taken another stride closer, and his

hand was outstretched toward the horse when the Black struck out savagely with his forefoot. The blow fell far short of its mark, but the policeman jumped back quickly, his face livid with anger.

"He tried to kick me," he yelled, still retreating. "You get him out of this park, and keep him out. He's a vicious animal and if I catch him around here again, I'll do more than give you a summons to appear in court!" Turning, he walked away hurriedly.

After the police car had gone, Alec led the Black along the bridle path until the fire had left the stallion's eyes. He took another look at the summons before shoving it angrily in his pocket and remounting the Black. If he appeared in court the following day, there would most likely be reporters around, and they would be more familiar with his name than the cop had been. Using Alexander, instead of Alec, wouldn't fool them, and the subsequent publicity could well lead to public knowledge that the Black was once again in the United States.

He had let Henry down, and he didn't even have the satisfaction of knowing the Black could beat Satan. He was confused, worried and angry with himself. But he realized there was no backtracking now. He would have to do everything possible to keep the Black's identity from the press.

Guilty!

7

Early the following afternoon, Alec walked from his home to the courthouse in downtown Flushing. He stopped before the building and his hand found the summons deep within his pocket. He didn't have to look at it again to know where to go. His offense of galloping a horse in a public park was classified by the Police Department as a traffic violation, and he was ordered to appear before the Traffic Court at two o'clock. It was two now.

Without moving forward, he watched the people hurrying into the building, some of them already holding their summonses in hand. Alec felt for the wallet in his hind pocket. He had twenty-five dollars there, and he knew that it would be more than enough to pay the fine. He should be getting inside now; no use putting it off any longer. If Dad had been along, it would have made things easier. But he had decided not to tell his father what had happened. He had assumed full responsibility when he had taken the Black to the park, and now he had to go through with it . . . alone. If he wasn't recognized, he'd pay the fine and no one would be the wiser.

But what if he was recognized? What would he do? What could he do? Alec walked toward the steps. He didn't know. There was no sense in thinking about it now. He would have to wait and see.

He followed the crowd inside the building. They were all going to the same room as he. They went up a flight of stairs, the well-worn wooden steps creaking beneath their combined weight. A policeman stood at the head of the stairs, directing them down the corridor. Alec followed the others into a large room where a dark-cloaked judge was presiding on the bench. The court was already in session, and Alec took a seat in the back of the room.

A police sergeant stood in front of the judge's bench, calling off the names of traffic violators; one at a time they went forward, pleading guilty or not guilty to the court's charge. If they admitted their guilt, they went to the cashier and paid their fine. If they believed themselves innocent, they pleaded not guilty and retired to one side of the courtroom, where later the judge would hear their defense.

While Alec waited for his name to be called, he looked around the crowded courtroom and wondered if among these people were any reporters from the newspapers. He knew that most editors assigned reporters to cover the city courts, hoping to pick up stories. One could be here now, but whether or not a court reporter would recognize his name was up to chance. Alec sat on a chair near the aisle; he was prepared to go to the bench promptly to avoid having his name called more than once by the sergeant.

He waited fifteen more minutes, listening to people plead guilty to speeding, overtime parking and going through red lights; then, suddenly, the police sergeant called, "Alexander Ramsay!"

It seemed to Alec that the sergeant's voice had risen to its highest pitch and that the room was much quieter than it had been since his arrival. He jumped up from his chair, tripped on a leg, caught himself, then hurried down the aisle. Reaching the sergeant, he looked up at him, his face white. Behind and above the sergeant he saw the judge.

". . . charged with galloping a horse in a public park. Guilty or not guilty?" The sergeant asked.

"Guilty," Alec said, but his voice was little more than a whisper.

"Guilty or not guilty?" the sergeant repeated.

"*Guilty!*" Alec shouted, and his voice thundered throughout the room.

The judge and sergeant were smiling as Alec walked to the cashier's desk.

He stood in line, very conscious of the many eyes upon him.

"You sure made no bones about it," the man in front of him said.

"About what?" Alec asked, moistening his lips.

"About your being guilty," the man replied, grinning. "You rocked the room like you meant it."

"I did?"

"You sure did." The man moved forward to pay his fine.

His hands trembling, Alec reached for his wallet. If only he could get out of here now. If he could just pay his fine and run. It seemed an hour before the man in front paid his fine and was gone. Now the cashier, too, was smiling as Alec faced him.

"That'll be fifteen dollars," the cashier said.

Alec gave the money to the man, and turned away hurriedly. With downcast eyes he moved toward the door. He slipped outside into the corridor, walking faster. He had reached the stairway, and his hand was on the rail, when a voice behind said, "Just a second, son."

He didn't stop or look around until he felt a hand grasp his arm. A slight man in a gray suit stood there.

"I'm from the *News*," he said. "You're Alec Ramsay, the jockey, aren't you?"

Alec jerked his arm from the man's grasp and continued down the stairs. But the man was beside him.

"Take it easy, Alec," he said. "All I want to know is why you've given up the track for riding hacks in a public park."

Alec reached the bottom of the stairs with the reporter still beside him. "Why weren't you up on Satan in Chicago? Henry Dailey told the press you weren't feeling well. How does that account for your galloping a horse in a public park at dawn?"

When Alec reached the door he burst into a run, and as he went outside and down the front steps of the building he heard the man shout, "I'll be seeing you, Alec."

Still running, Alec went down Flushing's Main Street. He weaved in and out among the people on the crowded sidewalk, unaware of their startled calls as he swept by, narrowly missing them.

He knew what the reporter would do. He'd call his city desk and acquaint his editor with what had happened in the

Flushing courthouse. His editor would in all probability send his sports reporter to follow up on the story. And, somehow, editors of other newspapers and press services would hear of it. They'd all come to Flushing . . . to the barn. They'd pin him down, and he'd have to answer their questions. He wouldn't be able to run away as he'd done from the police reporter.

He'd tell them he'd given up the track . . . that he wouldn't be riding Satan any more. That was the story they'd be after. But he wouldn't tell them it was the Black he had ridden in the park. They had no idea as to the identity of the horse he had ridden, and he wasn't going to help them find out!

Twenty minutes later Alec turned down his block, and his running strides lengthened as the barn came into view. He passed his house, going directly to the iron gate. As he pulled it open, he knew what he was going to do, and he didn't have any time to lose. The reporters would be here within an hour, maybe less.

The Black neighed shrilly as he opened the barn door, but for once Alec passed him by. He ran to the end of the barn, stopping before the bales of straw piled high against the wall. Taking one bale, he carried it to the door of the tack room and set it down on the floor. He went inside the room, removing the old chest and the chairs. When he had the room clear, he carried the bale of straw inside and with a pitchfork spread it about the floor. He went back for another bale and spread this, too, until the bedding was high. Then he got a bale of hay and placed it in a far corner of the room.

It was only then that he went to the Black's stall. The stallion came to him. "I'm going to move you for a while,"

Alec said, ". . . just for a little while."

Taking the Black by the halter, he led him from the stall. They went down the barn toward the tack room, the stallion's eyes shifting curiously. The Black stopped before the door, refusing to go inside. Patiently Alec waited, talking to him all the while.

"I know you'd like to go out in the field," Alec said anxiously. "But you'll have to wait until later . . . maybe tonight."

The stallion snorted, his eyes large and wondering.

Alec moved in front of him, and stood inside the room. "Come on, fellow," he said. "You'll like it in here . . . there's plenty of room, much more than in your old stall."

Abruptly the stallion moved, following Alec inside the tack room. The boy let go of his halter and stood in the doorway while the Black moved curiously about the room, the heavy straw silencing the sound of his restless hoofs.

Alec remained there until the Black found the hay in the corner and began to eat; then he left the room, closing the door behind him. There was still much to be done. Alec ran the length of the barn and went outside. He returned almost immediately, pushing a wheelbarrow to the Black's empty stall. Working hurriedly, he piled it high with the straw the stallion had used for bedding and wheeled it out to the manure pile in back of the barn. It took two more trips before the stall was clean of straw; then Alec removed the water pail from the corner of the stall and set it outside.

There was no evidence now that the stall had been occupied only a few minutes ago. From all appearances, there was only one stall being used in the barn and that, he would tell the reporters, was used by Napoleon.

Alec listened for any sound of the Black in the tack room. But the barn was still, and he knew that only a nicker or snort from the Black would give his presence away. Alec's plan was to keep the reporters away from the barn, except for a quick look, if they insisted, to see that only one stall was being used. The reporters, he figured, would be more interested in questioning him about his retirement from the track, and he would be able to keep them outside.

Alec glanced at his wrist watch. It was four o'clock. He could expect them any time now. But he was about ready for them; there were just a couple more things to do.

Filling the water pail, Alec took it to the tack room and hung it on a peg near where the Black was eating; then he got some feed, just to make sure the stallion would have enough to eat to keep him occupied for the next hour or so.

As he stood beside the Black, he heard the creaking of the iron gate. Quickly he turned away from the stallion and left the tack room, this time snapping the padlock on the door and placing the key in his pocket.

He was hurrying to the barn door when he heard the sound of hoofs on the gravel driveway . . . hoofs and the turning wheels of Tony's cart. The tenseness left his body as he realized it wasn't the reporters after all.

"Allo, Aleec," Tony called, when he saw the boy standing in the doorway. "Why you no put your Black in the field today?"

Alec waited until Tony had laboriously descended from the cart seat before going to him. "I need your help, Tony," he said anxiously. "I'm in a jam."

Tony's bright eyes turned quickly to him. "You need my

help? I give it to you. But what for you in this-a jam?"

"I took the Black to the park yesterday morning," Alec explained. "A cop saw us and I was given a ticket for galloping in a public park. This afternoon I went to court and a reporter there recognized me. I got away from him, but I'm sure others will be here very soon. I don't want them to know it was the Black I rode."

Tony's gaze turned from Alec to the barn. "But if these men come like you say, how you hide such a big horse, Aleec?"

"I have him in the tack room," Alec said. "I don't think they'll look around the barn much. They'll be more interested in questioning me."

"But what you want for me to do, Aleec?"

Alec went to Napoleon. "I'd like to put Napoleon in the field, and have you stay with me until they come. When they ask me what horse I was riding in the park, I'll tell them it was Napoleon. You can back me up."

Tony shook his head. "You think they believe you?"

"Why not?" Alec asked. "All they know is that I was given a summons for galloping. It could have been Napoleon as well as any other horse."

Shrugging his shoulders, Tony helped Alec unharness the gray. "Maybe it will work, Aleec. Maybe."

They had put Napoleon in the field, and were closing the gate, when they saw a car come to a stop before the iron fence.

"Here they are," Alec said, his gaze quickly returning to Tony.

"What we do now, Aleec?"

"Nothing. Just stay here. Let them come to us. We'll try to keep them away from the barn."

Tony turned again to the road. "There's-a two more cars stopping behind the first," he said.

Their eyes remained on Napoleon as the gate creaked open and the sound of many footsteps came toward them. They didn't turn to the newcomers until one said, "Hi, Alec."

There were six of them, and Alec recognized every one of them from interviews he'd had at the track. They were sports reporters sent by their editors to follow up the lead that the police reporter had uncovered. And now they leaned casually upon the fence, watching Napoleon as though it were their custom to drop in daily on Alec Ramsay.

But finally one of them asked, "Who's the horse, Alec?"

"That's Napoleon. Tony's horse," Alec said quietly. His eyes remained on the old gray as Napoleon plodded heavily across the field to better pasture. He waited for the reporters to ask him about his appearance in court, but the minutes went by without any one of them showing the slightest interest. The sound of footsteps on the driveway came again, and they all turned simultaneously.

A tall, heavy-bodied man came toward them, and Alec recognized Jim Neville, the foremost racing columnist in the country. Jim Neville had been Alec's friend for a long while. It was he who had been responsible for getting the Black into his first and only race in America.

Jim waved to Alec, then leaned on the fence with the others. "How've you been, Alec?" he asked.

"All right," the boy said quietly.

The reporter next to him said, "We figured you were sick. Out in Chicago, Henry Dailey said you weren't feeling well. That's why Lenny Sansone was up on Satan."

"I—I haven't been feeling too good," Alec said quickly.

"He's-a been taking it very easy," Tony added helpfully.

"But you've been doing some riding in the park to keep in trim. Is that it, Alec?" another reporter asked.

"That's it," Alec said.

"It makes a good story . . . you being top jockey, I mean, and then being picked up for racing in a public park," the reporter added.

"We weren't racing," Alec corrected him. "Just galloping a little."

"Who were you up on?" another asked.

Without hesitation, Alec said, "Napoleon there."

They all looked at the old gray for several minutes before one of them broke the silence by asking, "He gallops?"

"Sure," Alec said with feigned lightness.

"He's-a one fast horse," Tony added angrily. "Maybe he no look it, but Nappy he's-a fast all right."

"Sure, I believe you," the reporter said. "You can't go by looks. I know that for sure."

Jim Neville left the fence, walking a little to the rear of the reporters. "I haven't been around here in a long while, Alec," he remarked casually.

The others turned away from Napoleon to look about them; as one, their heads turned in the direction of the barn.

"How much room do you have in there, Alec?" one asked.

"Two stalls," Alec said. "But Napoleon has the place to himself."

"Mind if we take a look inside?"

"No . . . not at all."

The group walked toward the barn with Alec leading the way.

"It's funny the way cops can get mixed up," someone said. "We got hold of the cop who gave you the summons and he said you were up on a black horse . . . a big black, he said."

Alec's lips tightened, and it was Tony who said, "He's-a color blinded all right. Nappy is no black."

"He certainly isn't," the reporter agreed.

"But the cop said," another added casually, "that he'd never seen a horse run as fast as this one had gone."

"Nappy he's-a fast horse like I tell you," Tony said, laughing. "Maybe I race him one of these days. Maybe I do."

Alec said nothing. Now he realized that he had forgotten completely that the reporters could have interviewed the cop before coming here. They were looking for a bigger story than his retirement from racing. And that's why they wanted to go into the barn. From what the cop had told them they knew it couldn't have been Napoleon he had ridden in the park. Even now, they might suspect it was the Black! For what other horse could have kept him from riding Satan in Chicago? They knew he hadn't been sick at all. He had been silly to think he could keep the Black's identity from them. He had made the critical mistake of taking the Black to the park. Now he had to pay for it.

Alec stepped inside the barn, followed by the reporters. Jim Neville stayed at his side, but the others went directly to the stall the Black had occupied. They took one look at the clean-swept floor and then went on to Napoleon's stall. After that their gazes swept about the barn.

No sound came from the tack room, but any second the stallion could utter a snort that would betray his presence. Alec felt Jim Neville's hand upon his arm, but he didn't turn to him. The reporters had filed their way to the tack room, and already one of them was fingering the lock. Tony was with them, and Alec heard him say, "There's nothing in there; only harness for Nappy. We go outside now, yes?"

But the reporters weren't leaving. They had found what they sought; their gazes turned to Alec as one of them jiggled the lock. It was then that the stallion neighed.

"It's the Black, isn't it, Alec?" Jim Neville asked quietly.

Wearily Alec nodded.

"We all guessed it was, for the cop described him pretty well. Besides, we figured no other horse could have kept you off Satan in Chicago."

Now the reporters were asking for the key to the room. They wanted to see the Black to make sure it was he before writing their stories.

Alec walked toward the door, the key in his hand. It mattered little what happened now, for within a few hours the world would know that the Black was once again in the United States. The reporters were asking him many questions and he replied quickly and in as few words as possible. He told them that the Black belonged to him, that Abu Ishak was dead and had bequeathed the stallion to him. He wasn't going to race the Black. He and Henry had bought a farm. They were taking the Black there within two weeks.

And when he had answered all their questions, he inserted the key in the lock, knowing that they would go as soon as they had seen the stallion. He wanted them to go, to leave him alone with his horse.

The reporters stepped back when he opened the door. The Black was standing there, his eyes large and shifting. Alec held him by the halter while the reporters took one look at the giant stallion and then hurriedly left the barn.

Only Jim Neville remained when Alec led the stallion from the tack room. Tony walked beside the boy, but said nothing.

"I'm going to put him in the field, Tony."

Outside, the huckster ran ahead to open the gate. Napoleon looked up from his grazing and neighed at sight of the Black.

Alec released the stallion, and the Black burst into full gallop, passing Napoleon, who turned and trotted ponderously after him.

"I'm sorry, Aleec," Tony said.

"I was crazy to think I could keep it from them," Alec returned bitterly. "It's all my fault, Tony . . . no one else's."

"What happens now, Aleec?"

"I don't know, Tony. I really don't."

Abu Ishak's Promise

8

Tony shifted uneasily, for he didn't know whether or not Alec wanted him to stay around. The boy looked intently at the stallion, following his every move; yet Tony noticed that his eyes were sad. Finally the huckster glanced at Jim Neville, who now sat on the bench outside the barn.

"Why he not go like the others?" Tony asked angrily. "What more he want?"

Without turning from the field, Alec said bitterly, "He's a columnist, Tony. He's after the human-interest angle. The others take care of the straight news story, but Jim wants more than that. He wants to know how I feel and why.

". . . He wants to dig."

"I give it to him then," Tony said furiously. "I make him go quick!" Tony moved away from the fence, but Alec stopped him.

"I didn't mean it the way it sounded," Alec said. "It's his job, and he's a good friend. I can't run away any more. Tomorrow, when the stories break, we'll have plenty of visitors."

With Tony beside him, Alec walked toward the barn.

"You want me to stay, Aleec?"

"No, Tony. I'll get along with Jim all right. If you want to go home, I'll take care of Napoleon for you."

Tony left Alec at the barn, and the boy went to the bench, sitting down beside Jim Neville.

"He looks good, Alec," Jim said, his eyes on the Black. "He hasn't changed a bit. How does he go?"

"The same," Alec replied, his gaze too on the stallion. "Exactly the same."

"He might be just a little bit heavier."

"Maybe," Alec said. "But he could take that off."

"Yes, I suppose he could," Jim returned. "He was a fast one, Alec."

"He still is."

"Moves nicely, does he?"

"Perfectly."

Jim Neville was silent for a few moments, then he said, "He'll get some good colts for you, Alec. Satan is proof of that. I guess you'll be doing all right."

Alec nodded. "I hope so, Jim. We're going to buy the best mares we can get."

"Fine! Where's the farm, Alec?"

"Upstate . . . a hundred miles or so."

"Cyclone and Sun Raider have been retired to stud, too. But I guess you know that," Jim added quickly.

"Yes, I do."

"Remember how the Black whipped them both in the Chicago match race, Alec? Only four years ago, but it seems more like forty. You and Henry sure have come a long way since then."

"But we couldn't have done it without your help, Jim," Alec said gratefully.

The columnist laughed. "I wouldn't say that, Alec. All I did was to let the public know what you and Henry had to race; the people saw to it that the Black got in the match race. Too bad that was the only time they ever saw him race, though," he added thoughtfully. "I guess everyone who loves horses regretted that. A pity. A great pity."

Removing his hat, Jim placed it on the bench beside him, then turned to the field. "Look at him go, Alec," he said, nodding at the stallion, who had left Napoleon and was galloping down the field. "He certainly has Satan's action. Or, rather," he corrected himself, "Satan has his." He paused and without turning to the boy asked, "You've been up on them both, Alec. What do you think?"

"I don't get you, Jim."

"Which is the faster?"

"I couldn't tell you that," Alec said, rising. "I don't know." The Black was coming up the field and Alec started toward the gate, followed closely by Jim Neville.

"The Black could have been at his peak as a three-year-old," Jim suggested cagily.

"I don't think so," Alec replied, going to the fence, where the Black stood awaiting him. He placed his hand on the stallion's nose and stroked him until the Black snorted at Jim Neville and moved away.

The newspaperman leaned on the wooden rails with Alec.

"I don't suppose you've even considered racing him again?"
he asked. "Before you retire him, I mean."

"No."

"Maybe you should," Jim suggested. The boy turned to
him, but Jim Neville kept his gaze on the stallion and continued, "You'll be getting a lot of pressure to race him, you
know. Once the stories break tomorrow, there won't be anyone in the country who won't remember what the Black did
in his one and only race here. They'll want to see him run
again. You'll not have much peace, Alec."

"I'm not racing him, Jim," Alec said determinedly. "And
I'll take him away from here as soon as I can."

For a few minutes Jim Neville was quiet, and his large
frame leaned heavily against the rails. "You know," he said,
changing the subject, "I thought I'd never see a horse run as
fast as the Black. But I have," he added.

"You mean Satan?" Alec asked.

Nodding, Jim Neville said, "His one fifty-eight at Chicago
was something to see. When he opened away in the upper
stretch, I knew that this was the horse of all time."

"You don't think the Black could do better than one
fifty-eight?"

"No, do you?" Jim Neville turned from the stallion to
look at Alec.

"Yes, I do think so."

"Why don't you race him then, Alec?" Jim's words came
fast; he was taking advantage of Alec's pride in the speed of
the Black. "I'd like to see it. . . . So would everyone else."
He paused. "Don't you think you owe it to racing?"

Alec didn't reply.

"I remember the time you wanted nothing more than to

race the Black. It wasn't so long ago," Jim reminded Alec.

"It was different then."

"Why?" Jim Neville asked insistently. "Is it because you now have Satan racing?"

"No, Jim," Alec said quickly. "It's rather because I *have* raced Satan. I know what it means to lose your horse to the public. I'm not going to lose the Black to anyone. He's mine and I intend to keep it that way."

"But you haven't lost Satan," Jim said.

"It's hard to explain what I mean, Jim. I want to have my horse for myself. I want to take care of him. I want him to be mine and no one else's. Perhaps you'll call it selfishness, and I guess it is. But that's the way I feel. You can't make a pet of a champion racer, as Henry has often told me . . . and as I've found out for myself. You're bound to lose him to the public, no matter how hard you try. I don't want to lose the Black as I did Satan."

"So that's why you're retiring him to stud?"

Alec nodded. "That and because I want to have a lot of colts around, Jim . . . *his* colts. I want that kind of a life."

"Sure, I know," Jim said in a softer tone. "But can't you see your way clear to race him just once more before his retirement? I really think you should consider it for a number of reasons . . . and I say this as a friend and not a newspaperman looking for a story."

Alec turned to look searchingly at Jim Neville's large, ruddy face. "But what good would it do to race him just once more, Jim?"

"A lot of good, Alec. First of all, it would satisfy the craving of a lot of people who would like to see him race again . . . and others, too, who have just heard of the Black and never quite believed there was anything like him. You make it plain to all that this is his last race before retirement and everyone will be resigned to it and be grateful for their last chance to see the Black run. Human nature works that way, Alec. Whether the Black won or lost, you'd be the winner. They'd leave you alone."

"You still think Satan could beat him, Jim?"

"I do, Alec."

The boy turned to the field, while Jim Neville went on, "You should also consider the fact that if you're going to make breeding horses your livelihood, you'll probably be breeding mares other than your own to the Black. Racing him once more will give all racehorse owners a chance to see him in action, and when the time comes that you want to breed outside mares to the Black, you'll be able to command a good price for his services. You have to think of things like that, Alec, if it means your bread and butter and staying in the business you love. Whether you like to think of it or not," he added quietly.

The stallion came up the field toward them, and Alec slipped through the rails to go to meet him. He ran his hands down the long neck, lifting the heavy mane to scratch beneath it. He stayed there for many minutes before finally going back to Jim Neville.

"I don't believe Satan or any horse in the world could match strides with him," he said.

Jim smiled. "You mean you'll race him, Alec?"

Alec shook his head. "No, Jim. I'm going to take him away, just as I'd planned."

Shrugging his broad shoulders, Jim said, "He's your horse, Alec, to do with as you like." He paused before adding,

"But there's something else you should know about before I leave. It might make things a little more difficult for you, so it's only right that you should be prepared for it." The columnist removed a folded sheet of paper from his coat pocket. "I have here a list of the horses entered in the International Cup race. I managed to get the list before any other sportswriter . . . but they'll all have it tomorrow."

Jim Neville unfolded the paper before continuing. "You know, Alec, there won't be another race to equal this one. It's been more than a year in the making. The Association sent invitations to the owners of the world's fastest racers many months ago. This is a list of those horses whose owners accepted the invitations, and they'll all be in the United States next month."

"I know about the race," Alec said impatiently. "Satan was invited to run in it. Henry sent in his entry right after the Belmont."

"Yes," Jim Neville said without taking his eyes from the list, "his name is here all right. Like to know what his competition will be?"

"Sure."

"Well, there's Phar Fly, the Australian wonder horse; and Cavaliere, who won the Italian Derby in May; from India they're sending Kashmir, who won the Epsom Derby in England last year; and this year's Epsom Derby winner is coming here, too—that's Sea King, a British-bred colt, who is as highly thought of in England as Satan is here; then from France comes Avenger, who has won both the Irish and French Derbies this year; and from Argentina we'll have El Dorado, who has whipped just about everything in South America; then there's . . ."

"But what has this race to do with the Black, Jim?" Alec interrupted.

"A lot," Jim Neville said, lifting his eyes from the paper to meet those of the boy. "His name is here, too. He was entered by his owner, Abu Ishak of Arabia, six months ago."

The blood drained from Alec's face, and he stood before Jim Neville, dazed and silent.

"Abu Ishak had planned to race the Black in the International, Alec. In all probability he was going to ask you to ride him."

Alec said nothing, and after a long while he turned to the field.

"If you remember," Jim Neville went on, "Abu Ishak promised to bring the Black over here to race. It looks as if he had intended to keep his promise." The columnist paused before adding, "When this list is released tomorrow simultaneously with your story, the public will just expect you to keep the Black in the International. They'll figure you owe it to them."

Alec found his voice. "Not to them," he said quietly, "but to Abu." Meeting Jim Neville's gaze, he asked, "Abu wanted it that way, didn't he? He wanted to race the Black in the International Cup. He was going to keep his promise to race the Black here. I should have known he would."

"Since Abu Ishak had entered the Black in the race," Jim Neville said, "I'm sure that the Association will consider the Black as his entry and allow you to ride him even though he belongs to you now."

"Yes," Alec said slowly, "I suppose they would."

"Then you'll race him?"

"What else can I do, Jim? Abu wanted him to race in the International . . . so that's the way it's going to be regardless of how I feel about it. It's the least I can do . . . for him."

The Black's Public

9

Early in the afternoon of the following day Alec sat in his bedroom before an open window. Outside, the scene was far different from the tranquil one that had met his gaze until this day. For along the fence and far across the sidewalk and into the street were gathered hundreds of people waiting to see the Black.

Since early morning they had come, and Alec had been escorting two persons at a time into the barn. Now, while he took a rest, his father stood beside the locked gate, explaining to the crowd that the Black was too excited to be put in the field for all to see, and that they would have to wait for Alec to take them into the barn.

The newspapers which were responsible for it all were strewn about the room, and the sports page headlines read: "THE BLACK FOUND IN FLUSHING—Famous Sire of Satan Owned by Alec Ramsay" . . . "THE BLACK RETURNS TO

U.S.—Abu Ishak Bequeaths Stallion to Alec Ramsay." And there were others, all telling the world that he now owned the Black.

It was only Jim Neville who had the exclusive story of what lay ahead of them, and Alec turned to his column.

"Those of us," Jim wrote, "who saw the Black defeat Sun Raider and Cyclone four years ago at Chicago will never forget the tremendous speed of this giant stallion. With the years that have passed since that day, his spectacular victory has become to some a myth. So it is well that we shall all have the opportunity to see him race again. The Black is to start in the International Cup race to be held at the new racing plant just outside of Saratoga, New York, on the twenty-eighth of August.

"The Black will run as an entry from the Abu Ishak stable, for the Arab chieftain had entered him in the race. Alec Ramsay will, of course, ride him. It will be the Black's only race, for Alec Ramsay will retire him to stud immediately afterward. Whether or not the great stallion still retains the speed he had as a three-year-old remains to be seen. His competition will be the world's fastest horses, including his colt, Satan; Phar Fly, Australia; Avenger, France; Cavaliere, Italy; Sea King, England; El Dorado, Argentina; Kashmir, India . . ."

There was more, but Alec put the paper down to pick up the telegram that he had received earlier from Henry.

"Am at airport," Henry had wired from Chicago. "Don't do anything until I get there."

But he had done something. He had agreed to race the Black in the International. He wondered if Henry had read Jim Neville's column before sending the telegram. He doubted it, but knew Henry would have read it before he arrived at the barn.

Certainly Henry would understand! He was doing it for Abu Ishak. It was what Abu had wanted, and the Black would be in the International had the Sheikh lived. It was the least he could do for Abu, as he had told himself over and over again.

Alec went downstairs to find his mother in the living room. She was reading a newspaper, but let it fall to her lap when Alec appeared.

"Jim Neville says here that you're going to race the Black, Alec," she said, and her voice and face were heavy with concern although she tried hard to conceal her emotions.

"Just once more, Mom."

"But do you think that . . ." She stopped, well knowing that Alec understood what she meant to say.

He went to her and, bending, kissed her. "That it'll be all right?" he asked for her. "Sure it will."

"But the farm? You were going there with your father in a few days."

"We'll go right after the race," he said. "I've got to go through with it, Mom. You understand, don't you . . . as Dad does?"

"For Abu Ishak, you mean, Alec." She paused, smiling a little. "Yes, I guess I do." She turned to her paper again, and Alec left the room, not knowing she put the paper down again to watch him as he crossed the street.

The people pressed close to Alec as he went to his father at the gate.

"Just two at a time," Mr. Ramsay was saying. "Sorry, but we can't do any better than that." Opening the gate for

Alec, he said, "These two ladies are next, Alec."

Two women pushed through the gate with Alec, and he escorted them up the driveway. They were middle-aged, tall and lean.

"We live on the next block," one of them said, "so we're neighbors, Alec."

"It's perfectly thrilling to have a famous horse practically in our own back yard," said the other. "You must be so proud to have all these people here just to look at your horse," she added.

"Yes, ma'am," Alec replied. As he opened the barn door, he added, "I'm sorry, but you'll have to stay in the doorway. He's not used to visitors."

"All we want is a little peek," one said.

"Just to say we saw him," the other added.

The Black pushed his head over the stall door, whinnying at sight of Alec. Going to him, the boy rubbed him between the eyes and fed him a carrot.

"My, but he has a small head," one of the ladies called. "You'd never think it belonged to the rest of him."

A few minutes later Alec took the women back to the gate, where his father was waiting with the next two visitors. He knew that this would go on as long as the Black remained in Flushing.

It was several hours later when Alec saw Henry pushing his way through the crowd. His father had gone to the house for a rest, and the gate was locked and unattended. Reaching the gate, Henry put his hands on the bar and peered through.

"Alec!" he shouted. "Let me in!"

Alec moved his two visitors faster along the driveway until they reached the gate, which he opened for Henry.

Henry slipped inside, and shut and locked the gate behind him.

"No more visitors today!" the trainer called to the crowd, and his voice had an authoritative ring in it that the people didn't challenge. Taking Alec by the arm, he moved him quickly up the driveway. "This been going on all day?" he asked.

"Since eight o'clock," Alec said.

"How is he?"

"All right. No one got close to him."

They went into the barn, and Alec was on his way to the stallion when he heard Henry ask, "What's this story Jim Neville's got about your racing the Black in the International?"

Turning to Henry, Alec saw the concern so evident in his face. "Abu had entered the Black in the race," he said.

"I know that," Henry returned curtly. "I read the column. But did you actually tell Neville you'd go through with it?"

"Yes, I did, Henry. I felt I had to do it for Abu. He wanted it that way."

"What a guy wants and what he can actually have are two different things," Henry said quickly. "I don't care how much Abu wanted to see the Black in the International, he couldn't have raced that horse. How many times do I have to tell you, Alec, that the Black wasn't meant to set foot on a track with other stallions? Don't you believe me?"

Alec didn't reply, so Henry went on, "You're thinkin' that maybe you can handle him in spite of every- thing . . . the other stallions, the crowd, everything that goes along with a big race. Is that it?"

"I—I guess so, Henry."

"Maybe you can, Alec." Henry's voice was softer now.

"And then again, maybe you can't. I wouldn't like to watch you find out."

"But I did it in Chicago," Alec said quietly.

"You didn't, Alec," Henry corrected. "You had no control over him once he got on that track. He fought you, and you know that as well as I do. It was only by the grace of God that you weren't hurt and no one else was either. And he hasn't changed a bit since then . . . maybe he's worse for all we know. He's wild and uncontrollable under those conditions, Alec."

"Then you don't want me to race him in the International," Alec said.

"He's your horse. I'm just advising you not to do it. For your good as well as for the others in the race . . . and for the Black, too. Only harm could come of it." Henry paused. "He has all the natural speed in the world, Alec. But, as I've told you many times, his instinct is to fight other stallions, not race 'em. And what about the farm, Alec? What about all your talk?"

"But I *do* want the farm, Henry. I want to take the Black there more than anything else in the world. But don't you see," he pleaded, "I know now that Abu meant to race him in the International . . . that he made a promise he intended to keep. I feel it's my job to keep his promise for him." Alec paused. "And Jim Neville said, too, that I owed it to the sport . . . that it wouldn't be right to let the people down."

"Sure, he said that," Henry returned. "And maybe he's right. But they don't know the Black as well as we do. He could raise havoc on the track, and that wouldn't do the sport any good either. There are some mighty valuable horses in the International, Alec, an' I wouldn't want to be responsible for any damage done."

"And I wouldn't either, Henry," Alec said. "But maybe he won't act up at all. Maybe he'll do everything I ask of him." Alec's face became eager and excited as he added, "And if he runs, Henry, he'll show everyone that there's not another horse in the world like him!"

Henry closely scrutinized Alec's face. "So that's it, too. You think he can beat Satan as well as the others."

"I do, Henry. I really do."

"And it's in you to find out, just as I thought it was."

"What do you think, Henry? Could Satan beat him?" The Black pushed his muzzle toward Alec's pocket, seeking a carrot.

"It's not fair to ask me that, Alec," Henry said, after a long silence. "You know how I feel about Satan."

"You mean you're closer to him than to the Black."

"Guess you can call it that. I've done something with Satan. He has the Black's speed and he'll turn it off an' on for anyone on his back. It's a combination hard to beat . . . for *any* horse," he added, turning to the stallion.

"Henry," Alec began slowly, "let's take the Black to the International track for training. If between now and the day of the race he gives me any trouble, you just say the word, and we'll withdraw him."

"You'll let me decide then, Alec? You promise that if I think he's going to create a lot of trouble you won't race him? Is that our agreement?"

"That's it, Henry. Whatever you say goes."

"Okay, Alec," Henry said, extending his hand, which the boy clasped. "We'll do it. We'll take him to the track to-

morrow and start working him. None of the other horses
will be there yet, and Satan won't be shipped from Chicago
until next week. So we'll have the place to ourselves for a
while, which is good. I'll stick with you all along, but remember our agreement. If I say he's out of the race, he's
out."

Nodding, Alec turned to his horse. "You're going to the
races, Black. You're going to have one last crack at all of
them . . . and you'll give them something to remember
you by, long after you're at the farm."

The stallion neighed, and Alec flung his arms around the
sleek neck.

International Track

10

It was dark the next morning when the van went down the driveway, with Henry driving and Alec beside him. In the back was the Black, his legs well bandaged to prevent injury during the long trip ahead. He was halter-tied close to the small open window of the driver's cab, and Alec was able to reach through it and touch his horse.

Long before it became light they had driven through New York City's empty streets; and they were well on their way to Albany when the first streaks of dawn creased the sky.

"How much longer, Henry?" Alec asked.

"We won't be there till around noon," Henry replied, without taking his eyes from the road. "No hurry. Have to take it slow with him."

"I know. I was just wondering when we'd be there." Reaching through the window, Alec fed the Black a carrot, then once more settled back in the corner of his seat.

After a long while Henry said, "The International track is about forty-five miles north of Albany. It's a new one, y'know. They've only just finished it."

"How come they're holding the Cup race there, Henry? Why not at Belmont or one of the other tracks close to a big city?"

"Because the International was their idea. And what better send-off could you give a new track than to sponsor such a race? I guess the track's board of directors figured it that way. And the International Cup race is just before their first regular meeting, so the people coming to the International will most likely stay on for the meeting." Henry switched off the van's headlights, for now it was light enough to see the road.

It was ten o'clock when they drove through Albany's heavy traffic and found their way out of the city, continuing to the north. Henry glanced at his watch. "Around noon we'll be there," he said, "like I told you."

The countryside became slightly rolling, and after a little while they were able to see the towering peaks of the Adirondack Mountains far in the distance. Alec settled back comfortably in his seat. "This is the way I like it," he said.

Henry glanced at him, then turned back to the road.

"I mean, just the three of us again," Alec explained. "The way it was when no one knew about us."

Nodding, Henry said, "I know, Alec. There's no thrill like bringing a horse along like we did the Black . . . and Satan, too . . . then springing him in a big race without anyone's knowin' what we had." Pausing, Henry looked at Alec again. "But once you do that, y'got to go along with the crowd."

The Black had his muzzle in the window and Alec rubbed

it, saying, "Anyway, I'm glad we're going to have a week alone. You said it'd be about a week, didn't you, Henry?"

"It should be, Alec. I learned that Phar Fly, the Australian horse, arrived in California yesterday, but they're not flying him east until next week. El Dorado, the South American champ, is already on his way, too; he'll be one of the first to arrive. The European horses and Kashmir, who was in England, are coming together; they'll arrive late next week, if they stick to the schedule released. And, as I told you, I'm having Satan shipped here early in the week."

"I wonder if they'll know each other."

"Who?"

"The Black and Satan."

Henry smiled. "No. They've forgotten all about each other. Satan was only a few months old when they were separated."

Alec turned to the Black. "Anyway, it's going to be interesting to watch them together."

"Yeah," Henry muttered. "Mighty interesting."

During the next hour they drove through many small towns and penetrated ever deeper into the Adirondack foothills.

"Just a few miles now," Henry said.

Alec was fingering his stopwatch, pressing the stem and following the second hand as it swept around the face. Finally he looked up at Henry. "Do you have your stopwatch with you?"

Henry's hand went to his pocket and he removed the watch, which he gave to Alec. The boy pressed both stems simultaneously.

"Think your watch is off?" Henry asked.

"I don't know. I just thought I'd check it."

When the hands of Henry's watch came to two minutes, Alec stopped both watches. He found the hands of his watch registering exactly two minutes also.

"What made you think it was off?" Henry asked, without turning to the boy.

"I just wanted to make sure it was right," Alec replied evasively.

Henry was silent for a few minutes; then he said thoughtfully, "You never did say why you took the Black to the park that morning the cop picked you up."

"You never asked me, Henry."

"Well?"

"I wanted him to stretch out."

Henry turned to the watches Alec held in his hand. "For any particular reason?" he asked.

For a minute Alec was undecided whether or not to tell Henry; then he said, "He did it in one fifty-nine, Henry."

Henry kept his eyes on the road as he said, "From the seventh tee to the elm tree?"

"A mile and a quarter, isn't it, Henry?"

"It's that, all right. We measured it together."

"The bridle path is pretty soft and deep," Alec said quietly.

"Yeah, I know."

"And it was the first time in a long while he's stretched out."

"I realize that, too, Alec."

"What are you thinking?"

"It's going to be mighty close, if the Black races."

"With Satan?" Alec asked.

"Mighty close," Henry repeated. And that was all he said.

They were silent after that, each alone with his thoughts. Finally they saw the great grandstand and buildings of the International track.

The stallion struck his hoof soundly against the side of the van, and Alec turned to him. "Just a few more minutes now," he said.

They drove along the high fence for a few miles before coming to the barn entrance of the track. Henry turned into it and drove the van up the tree-lined road that wound its way toward the stables. Some workmen landscaping the grounds stopped to watch them as they drove by. A short distance farther on was a white wooden-framed building, and Henry brought the van to a stop before it.

"Must be the offices," he told Alec. "I'll find out which stalls we're in."

After Henry had left, Alec turned to kneel upon the seat and press his cheek against the Black as the stallion pushed his muzzle through the window. Alec felt the stallion's quivering lips and said, "We're here, Black. You're going to take it easy, aren't you? You won't give me any trouble as Henry thinks you will."

Alec was still talking to the Black when Henry reappeared and climbed into his seat. "Stalls Nine and Ten in Row C," he said.

As the van started forward Alec settled back in his seat again. They passed the long stands and went toward the many rows of sheds a half-mile away.

"We're the first here, just as I thought we'd be," Henry said.

Now, with the great stands behind them, they were able to see the track, and Alec looked at it for a long time before turning to the green infield with the lake in the center, over which glided a small group of white swans.

Bordering the track at the far turn were the sheds, and as they neared them Henry asked, "What row was it?"

"C," Alec told him. "Stalls Nine and Ten."

They passed rows A and B, and turned down C.

"I guess they're figuring on putting all the horses running in the International in this row," Henry said.

Stalls 9 and 10 were only a short distance down the row, and Henry stopped the van before them. First out of the cab, Alec went to the bales of straw piled high beside the stall door. "Which stall will we put him in, Henry?"

"Either one," Henry called back. "We'll use the other for bunking down in until Satan gets here. But let's get the tack out first," he added.

They opened the back door of the van, pulling out the ramp. Whinnying, the Black moved his hindquarters uneasily and tried to turn his head toward them, but the rope held him close. Going into the van, Alec spoke to him and went to the tack trunk, which he pushed toward the door. Henry took hold of it, carrying it into Stall 9. Alec followed him, carrying the pitchforks, and went to the bales of straw. He took one and spread the straw about the stall. When he had finished, Henry had the pails and feedbags off the van.

"I guess we're about ready for him now," Henry said.

Carrying a lead shank, Alec went into the van. "Whoa, boy," he said, walking to the side of the Black; and his hand ran over the stallion's body. He fed the Black a piece of carrot before untying the ropes and snapping the lead shank onto his halter. Slowly he turned the stallion and led him to the ramp.

The Black pricked his ears far forward as he looked out of the van, and he hesitated at the ramp while Alec stepped upon it. "There's nothing here to bother you," the boy said, breaking off another piece of carrot and giving it to the Black.

The stallion stepped onto the ramp, then stopped again, while Alec waited, talking to him all the while. Curiously the Black moved his head about, his eyes constantly shifting.

"No, it's not home," Alec said. "We're a long way from there." His hand moved down the long neck as he talked. He gave the Black another piece of carrot, making him reach for it. The Black moved forward again until his hindlegs came to the ramp; he stopped once more and Alec waited. Finally Alec moved farther down the ramp, holding out another carrot for the stallion. The Black reached for it, and as Alec moved away, the stallion let himself go, his hindquarters firmly gathered beneath him as he followed the boy down.

When the Black reached the ground, Alec gave him the carrot, then waited again while the stallion turned to the left, then to the right, looking at everything there was to see.

Henry came up, carrying a pail of water. The Black turned to him, his lips quivering; then he pushed his muzzle into the pail.

Alec said, "I'll walk him up and down the row a bit, Henry. It'll get him loosened up and used to the place at the same time."

Nodding, Henry watched Alec lead the stallion down the row toward the road. He saw the Black shy away from a power motor that a workman had left running near one of the stalls. But Alec moved with him, then brought him to a stop. A minute later he was leading the stallion to the mower, letting him sniff it to find out it was nothing to fear or fight.

Henry went into the van to get the two folded cots they were to use as their beds; then he removed the blankets from the trunk and hung them over a line to air.

Alec was bringing the stallion up the row when Henry turned to them again. The Black saw the blankets waving in the breeze and came to a stop, snorting. His eyes never left the blankets as he pawed the earth with his forefoot.

"Only a couple of blankets," Alec said softly. He waited a few minutes, then moved the Black toward them. The stallion snorted repeatedly and his lips curled, but he moved quickly beside Alec. Stopping just before the blankets, Alec let the stallion go to them. The Black sniffed them, and then after a few minutes turned away.

"Everything is strange to him now," Alec told Henry. "But he'll get used to it." He paused. "I'll walk him to the track now, and let him take a good look at it."

Henry joined Alec as the boy led the stallion up the long row. When they reached the end, they were near the far turn of the track, and the homestretch going past the grandstand stretched before them.

"It's a nice, clean racing plant," Henry said. "The track looks mighty good."

"Shall we walk around it, Henry?"

"If you want. It's a good idea to know what we'll be running over."

"Shall we take him with us?"

Henry turned to the stallion, standing quietly beside Alec. "I guess it'll be all right."

"The sooner he gets used to it the better," Alec said.

They left the row and went to the gate leading onto the track. "Keep a good hold of him now," Henry said as they walked through the gate. "Let's get over near the rail."

With his neck highly arched, the Black stepped lightly beside Alec, sometimes moving a few strides ahead of him and pulling a little. His head and eyes were in constant motion, turning to the empty stands on his right and to the green grass of the infield on his left.

"He'd like to go a little," Alec said as they went along.

"This walk oughta take some of it out of him," Henry replied, his eyes on the track. "Can you keep him down?"

"Sure. But he'd still like to go."

They moved slowly about the great oval, Henry's eyes leaving the track footing only to look at the Black.

"He wasn't any trouble at all," Alec said when they arrived back at the gate. "It's just as though he knows what this is all about."

"He seems all right now, Alec," Henry agreed. "But it's still too early to tell much."

"Would it be all right if I got up on him?" Alec asked eagerly.

"Y'mean now . . . without a bridle or saddle?"

"It doesn't make any difference to him."

"Or to you?" Henry asked.

"No bit can hold him when he wants to run. I can do as well without one."

Henry was silent for a while, then he said, "Go ahead, Alec, if you think it'll do him any good. You know him better than I do. But keep him to a slow gallop, if you can."

Alec moved to the side of the Black, raising his knee for

Henry to boost him onto the stallion's back. A quick heave by Henry and he was up, and the Black displayed no uneasiness.

His knees pressed firmly against the stallion, Alec leaned forward to unsnap the lead shank from the halter. "I won't need this," he told Henry, tossing it to him.

The trainer stepped back as the Black crabstepped, then went into a trot. Going to the outside rail, Henry leaned upon it, his eyes never once leaving Alec and the Black. He saw the boy's hands slip a little farther down the stallion's neck as he leaned forward. Obediently the Black moved closer to the inside rail and went into his long, loping canter as they passed the stands. Henry knew that the stallion was obeying Alec's every command; just now the boy had full control over him.

The stallion swept around the first turn, his strides gradually lengthening, his head carried high with ears pricked. But there was no wildness to his gait, no evidence of the fiery energy that Henry knew burned within him.

"Maybe Alec will be able to do it," he said. "Maybe he will."

They moved into the backstretch with Alec lost from Henry's sight, for the boy was low beside the Black's neck and covered by the long, flowing mane. The stallion's strides were long and effortless, yet every once in a while, for no apparent reason Henry could see, he would strike out playfully without breaking stride. His head would turn very often, too, to look to the left, then to the right of him.

"They could be out for a joy ride," Henry muttered. "Yet he's really moving, and without even tryin'." His hand went to the stopwatch within his pocket. "If Alec has that much control over him when the others get here, there'll never be a race to equal it."

They came around the far turn, and as they passed Henry, Alec waved to him. The stallion went down the stretch with his tail flowing behind him like a black cloak. Going into the first turn again, Henry saw the Black start to level out, and he knew Alec was letting him go.

There was no turning of head or striking of forefoot as the Black came off the turn. He was really moving now and his action was beautiful and breathtaking to see. Henry pressed the stem of his stopwatch when the Black passed the three-quarter pole. He pushed it again when the stallion swept by the quarter pole, then looked at his watch.

"Forty-five seconds flat for the half-mile!" he said aloud.

With thunderous, racing hoofs, the Black passed Henry once more, and this time Alec didn't wave to him. Henry saw that Alec was trying to bring the stallion to a stop.

When they went into the first turn the Black's strides were slowing, and by the time they had entered the backstretch again Alec had him down to a slow gallop, then to a trot.

Henry looked at his watch to make sure of the time in which he had caught the Black. He knew that Satan couldn't run a faster half-mile than the Black had just gone. He turned back to the stallion as Alec brought him slowly around the turn.

He's got the old speed all right, Henry thought. But I knew that. The question is, will he run or fight? And no one is going to answer that until the others get here. No one . . . not even Alec.

The Black Meets Satan

11

As the remainder of the week passed and Henry watched Alec take the Black through his daily gallops, he found himself thinking more and more about the possibility of the Black's actually running in the big race. Alec's control of the great stallion was impressive to watch, and the boy's enthusiasm and confidence were transmitted to Henry. It was only when the trainer was alone that he angrily reminded himself it was much too early for optimism . . . that the Black's willingness to do what Alec asked of him meant nothing until the Black caught the wind of other stallions. So it was that Henry looked forward anxiously . . . yet with a feeling of dread, too . . . to the day the others would arrive.

It came a day earlier than Henry had expected. He and Alec were driving back from town, where they had gone for their evening meal, when they saw the van ahead of them.

"Could it be Satan, Henry?" Alec asked anxiously.

"No. He's coming in tomorrow morning. Has to be one of the others. El Dorado is my guess."

"The South American horse?"

Nodding, Henry followed the van through the barn entrance gate, and pulled up beside it when it came to a stop before the barn office. "Who y'got?" he asked the van driver.

"El Dorado," the man replied.

Henry drove on. "Well, it's the beginning," he told Alec. "Things will change pretty fast around here from now on."

"You mean because we won't have the place to ourselves any longer."

"Yeah, mostly that," Henry mumbled.

They were back at the stall only a short time when the van turned down the row, coming to a stop just below them and on the opposite side. Suddenly the Black's shrill whistle shattered the air, and Alec and Henry turned to him.

He had his head stretched far over the door. His ears were pricked, almost touching at the tips, while his eyes were large and had a startled look. He whistled again and his forefoot struck heavily against the door.

"Shall I close the top of the door, Henry?"

"No, there's no sense in shutting him up. We've got to see what he'll do from now on. We've got to be sure, if we're going to race him."

Two men were taking El Dorado off the van. He was a light golden chestnut of medium height. He walked quietly alongside his handlers and his movements were frictionless.

"Supple as a cat, that one," Henry said. "And a lot of power to go along with it."

"But his racing records don't come anywhere near those of Satan," Alec said.

"No," Henry admitted, "nor of the others, either. We'll have to keep an eye on him . . . but no need to worry too much about him. It'll be Phar Fly and the European horses that'll give us the most trouble."

El Dorado stopped in his tracks when the Black whistled again. Snorting, he turned his golden head in the direction of the Black. He snorted again, then moved about uneasily; his handler led him down the row while the other man got his stall ready.

Alec went to the Black, but the stallion had eyes only for the chestnut. Alec stayed with his horse while Henry went to join the man walking El Dorado.

Repeatedly the Black struck his door. Alec offered him a carrot, but the stallion ignored it. Turning to El Dorado, Alec saw that the chestnut was becoming excited by the Black's frequent challenging whistles; the man at his head kept him far down the row, while Henry walked beside him.

A short while later El Dorado was led into his stall and Henry returned. "They're a little worried about their horse," he told Alec.

"You mean because of the Black?"

"No, not that. He wasn't feeling well a couple of days ago and ran a pretty high fever."

"But he's all right now, isn't he? He looks it, anyway."

"Yeah, they think so. No fever, and he's eating well. But they're going to keep a close watch on him."

With the coming of night the Black continued to remain at the door, watching for a glimpse of El Dorado and repeating his shrill, piercing blasts.

"I thought he'd get over seeing him by now," Alec said, while he and Henry sat on the bench outside the stall.

"Sometimes they never get over it," Henry answered quietly.

"But the Black will. I'm sure he will."

Shrugging his shoulders, Henry said, "Maybe, Alec. An' maybe not. But we'll know before long."

"Is Lenny Sansone coming with Satan?" Alec asked, intentionally changing the subject.

"Yeah, I thought it best if he worked him right along, Alec. I figured the Black wouldn't like to see you up on Satan even during the works."

"I guess you're right, Henry."

Long after they had gone to bed, Alec heard the Black's pounding against the door and the constant shifting of his feet as he moved uneasily about his stall.

Tomorrow there would be even more to occupy the stallion's mind, Alec knew. For tomorrow Satan would arrive. And after him would come Phar Fly, Cavaliere, Sea King, Avenger and Kashmir. Yes, as Henry had said, things were going to change pretty fast around there from now on.

The next morning Henry took the van to meet the plane bringing Satan, while Alec stayed behind to take care of the Black. He was grooming the stallion when one of the men who handled El Dorado appeared at the stall door.

"I wonder if you could loan us one of your pails?" the man asked. "El Dorado banged up ours yesterday."

"Sure," Alec said, leaving the stall.

The man followed him. "We're getting a couple more, so I'll return this to you by afternoon," he said when Alec gave him the pail. "That's some looking horse you have there," he added. "Heard a lot about him. Is he everything they say he is?"

"I think so," Alec said.

The Black had his head over the stall door and once more screamed at El Dorado, even though the chestnut wasn't in sight.

"Is he like that always?" the man asked.

"No," Alec replied.

"Give you any trouble?"

"No."

After the man had gone Alec finished grooming the Black, then turned to the adjacent stall, where the cots were. He was about to remove them to get the stall ready for Satan when he stopped to look thoughtfully at the Black. Perhaps it wouldn't be such a good idea to put Satan next to the Black. And there was no reason why they couldn't use Stall Number 8 for Satan; then their sleeping quarters would be between the two horses. It might be better that way until they saw how things worked out between Satan and the Black. Alec felt certain that Henry could fix things up at the office for the use of the extra stall.

He went to Stall Number 8 and bedded it down well for Satan; then, having some free time, he went across the row to get his first close look at El Dorado.

The man who had borrowed the pail was grooming the chestnut. He looked up when Alec appeared at the stall door.

"How is he?" Alec asked. "Henry told me that you were a little worried about him."

"He's all right now. Although your black horse has made him more nervous than I like to see him." He paused, turning to Alec. "You're sure you can handle that horse? I've seen fighting stallions before and he certainly seems to be one."

"I can handle him," Alec said.

"One like that can bring out the worst in any stallion," the man said, still unconvinced.

Alec was about to reply when he heard the van coming down the row. Leaving the stall, he saw Henry, accompanied by Lenny Sansone and Fred, the groom who took care of Satan. He waved to them as the van rolled by and came to a stop near their stalls.

Lenny Sansone, short and stocky and in his middle thirties, was the first off the van. He came toward Alec, a large grin on his wizened face, his hand outstretched. "It's good seeing you again, Alec."

"Good seeing you, too, Len," Alec replied, clasping the other's hand. "You've been really riding Satan," he added.

"I just sit there and let him go. You know him," Lenny said.

Henry and Fred were at the back of the van when Alec went to them. "How'd he ship, Fred?" he asked of the groom.

"Fine, Alec. Just fine," Fred grinned. "He takes to travelin' just like everything else. There's no more horse anywhere."

The back door of the van came down, and Satan neighed shrilly. Then the Black screamed, and his whistle was more piercing than Alec had ever heard it. He turned to him and saw that the stallion's eyes were bright with fury. Lenny Sansone, who was standing close to the Black's stall, called, "He's apt to tear this door down, Alec!"

Alec went to the Black, but the stallion's eyes never left

the van, for Satan stood at the ramp.

"Stay with him, Alec!" Henry shouted. He and Fred had Satan by the halter; the burly colt uttered a shrill scream and his ears swept back, flat and heavy against his head.

"He's never acted that way since I've known him," Lenny said. "It must be the Black."

The Black struck his foot hard against the door again, almost shattering the wood.

"Another blow like that and you won't have any door," Lenny warned.

Without fully realizing what he was doing, Alec pushed the Black's head back, then quickly opening the door he went inside. "Bolt it again, Lenny!" he called.

The stallion came back to the door, his eyes blazing, while Alec stood beside him. "Easy, Black. Easy," he pleaded. But the giant body continued to tremble in fury as Alec ran his hand over him. Alec stayed near the small, glaring head, desperately trying to keep the stallion from stepping too close to the door.

Henry was taking Satan down the ramp, but seeing Alec inside the stall he called angrily, "Get out of there, Alec!"

But the boy didn't hear him, for he was moving with the Black as the stallion turned furiously about the stall. He didn't think the Black would kick him, but he wasn't sure under these circumstances; so he kept close to the stallion's head, his hand resting lightly on the halter. Always he talked to his horse, coaxing, urging, guiding. But it seemed the Black didn't even know him now. Nothing but fury and hate absorbed the stallion.

The Black moved quickly toward the door again, carrying Alec with him. He struck high with his foreleg, bringing it down over the door. Outside Satan was rearing, and his face, too, was fearful to see.

Lenny Sansone had hold of the upper half of the stall door. "Get out, Alec! I'll shut it!" he shouted.

Knowing that he was afraid, Alec tightened his grip on the halter. If he left now, he knew he'd forever be afraid of the Black. Anything would be better than that. His heart pounding, he stepped in front of the stallion, trying to force him back from the door. His weight threw the stallion off balance and the Black pulled his foreleg off the door.

"Shut the top!" Alec shouted to Lenny.

"Not until you get out!"

"Shut it!" Alec shouted again, and when the door remained open for the Black to see what was going on outside, Alec pulled it shut himself.

The only light came through a small, high window to the rear of the stall. And within the light Alec moved with the Black, always talking to him, always touching him. The stallion screamed his piercing challenge repeatedly. For a while he was answered by Satan's whistle; then it was quiet outside and Alec knew that Henry and the others had moved Satan away from the Black's stall.

Gradually the stallion's actions became less furious. For a time he stood still and was responsive to Alec's voice and hands. But then he was on the move again, turning restlessly about the stall, stopping only to paw at the straw with his forefoot.

It was only after a long while that the fire left his eyes and he turned to Alec. He shoved his nose hard against the boy's chest, then nuzzled his pockets for carrots.

Removing one, Alec fed it to him. "You didn't want it

before," he said, "you didn't want anything but to fight. It can't work out that way, Black . . . not for you or for me. Neither of us belongs here if it's going to be that way. Maybe I've been wrong all along. . . . Maybe we shouldn't be here at all."

And as Alec remained with his horse he thought of how much he had looked forward to the day when the Black would meet his colt. He'd even thought they would recognize each other for what they were, father and son. But it hadn't worked out that way at all. There was no love between them. They were two giant stallions, both eager and willing to fight. No, it wasn't the same as he'd thought it would be at all. And now Alec wondered what he would do . . . and, more important, what Henry would do, for it was he who would decide whether or not the Black would race in the International.

Later Alec left the stall, closing the top door. He walked up the row to the end stall, where Henry stood alone, leaning on the door, watching Satan.

The black colt drew away from Henry when Alec joined the trainer. "How is he?" the boy asked anxiously, reaching out to touch Satan. But the colt moved farther back into his stall.

"He's calming down now," Henry said quietly. "He'll be all right."

Taking a carrot from his pocket, Alec held it out to Satan. The big colt took a step closer, his heavy head extended; but then he came to a stop again and his nostrils quivered.

"He probably smells the Black on you," Henry said. Alec was withdrawing his hand when Henry added, "Keep it there. He'll come over."

A few minutes later Satan took the carrot from Alec's hand and moved to the door, while the boy and trainer patted him.

"I'm sorry it had to happen this way," Alec said.

"I'm sorry, too," Henry returned.

"What are you going to do?"

"I don't know, Alec. Just now I don't think it's going to work out . . . as I said it wouldn't."

"Maybe the Black will get used to the others . . . within a few days, I mean."

"Maybe," Henry repeated.

"Then we'll keep him here and see?" Alec asked anxiously.

The trainer shifted uneasily on his feet. "I don't know, Alec . . . really, I don't. It might be better for everyone if we took him away now. Things might not get better an' they could get worse."

"But maybe . . ." Alec began.

"I'd like to see him race as much as you would," Henry interrupted. "More now than before we came here." Pausing, he added, "But you saw what he did to Satan, and he could do the same to the others. The Black brings out the instinctive savageness and hatred in every stallion to fight his kind. Up to now, these horses know but one thing an' that's to race as they've been trained to do. Racing is something the Black hardly knows anything about. . . . Fighting is what he knows best."

"Then what do you think we should do, Henry?"

"Let's wait a week for the others to get here. Let's make sure I'm right before we take him away. He just might come around, Alec, the way you think he will. . . . He just might."

Turning down the row to the Black's stall, Alec knew he wasn't really so sure that his stallion would come around. No, not at all. And perhaps both he and Henry were making a mistake in keeping the Black here for another week.

As Henry had said, things could get worse, much worse.

Fighting Stallion!

12

The following week saw the arrival of all the horses entered in the International Cup race. Phar Fly, the Australian champion—a robust blood bay stallion with glossy black mane, tail and stockings—was the first to arrive; then came the European horses. Sea King, from England, was a gray, small in height but long-bodied. Cavaliere, from Italy, was a rich brown stallion with four white stockings, standing seventeen hands in height. His entire physique signified power. Avenger, from France, was a round, chunky little dark bay horse, dainty to the point of femininity, his action effortless and birdlike. The last to arrive at the track was Kashmir, from India, a sorrel with white face and feet; sixteen hands strong he stood, alert and confident, high-spirited and fractious.

And with their arrival came the owners, trainers, exercise boys, grooms and reporters. No longer was the row quiet, belonging only to Alec and Henry, for now from morning until night horses and people filed up and down the row.

The top of the Black's stall door was left open for only a few hours each day. And during that time Alec and Henry would stand close by, watching him, ready for anything he might do.

"He's got to get used to seeing them around," Henry had said earlier in the week. "A few hours a day will be enough until we think he's ready to be with the others."

But the Black's hatred of the other stallions did not lessen with each passing day. His shrill challenging whistles were screamed constantly, even from behind closed doors.

A week before the big race, Alec stood beside Henry at the track rail, watching Lenny Sansone work Satan. Working out with the burly colt were Cavaliere and Avenger.

Satan was moving fast, coming down the backstretch, and Henry had his watch on him. The black colt swept thunderously into the turn, moving close to the rail. Leveled out, with his ears flat against his head, Satan came off the turn and passed them.

The light of a trainer's joy and pride in the part he had played in molding such a horse shone in Henry's keen gaze as he watched Satan. He pressed the stem of his watch and glanced at it. "He's ready. They'll have to really go to beat him," he said, making no attempt to keep his enthusiasm from Alec.

"What'd he do it in?"

"Forty-five."

"The Black went that," Alec reminded Henry.

"I know," Henry said. "But what good is his speed? What good is it, when we've got to gallop him nights and keep him penned up during the day?"

Cavaliere passed and they watched the big brown stallion who had won the Italian Derby as his rider let him out going down the stretch.

"His action is a lot like Satan's," Alec remarked.

"Yeah," Henry said, "but there's the one you want to watch, Alec." He was pointing to Avenger, as the small champion from France moved down the backstretch. "Round and dainty," Henry added, "but he sure can go. Look at that action, Alec. . . . That's what won him his big races!"

Avenger moved with long strides that belied his smallness. He glided over the track, scarcely seeming to touch it with his flying feet.

"He has the coordination of a machine," Henry said enthusiastically. "And he won't make any wrong moves, Alec. I'll have to tell Lenny to watch him; he's the kind of a horse who could slip by you without your even knowin' it."

Alec turned to his friend. "Henry, what are we going to do about the Black? We just can't go on like this. We've got to make up our minds. It's not fair to him."

"What do you think we should do, Alec?" Henry returned.

"I don't know. Sometimes I think he's just making a lot of noise . . . that he wouldn't fight at all if we took him out with the others. This is all so new to him that it's only natural he should be excited."

"I've been thinking along those lines, too, Alec. But we could both be wrong," Henry added.

"Or we could be right," Alec argued.

"Yes, I suppose we could."

"He was coming along well until the others got here."

"That's just it, Alec . . . until the others got here, and

they're still here. He's not making it easy for them, either."

"I know," Alec said. "But maybe if we gave him a chance he'd get it out of his system. He needs to work with the others." The boy paused, and added: "We'd know then, Henry. We could take him away if we were absolutely sure he wasn't going to come around. I'd feel all right about withdrawing him from the race, knowing we'd done all we could."

"You mean, if we did that, you'd feel that we'd done everything Abu Ishak could have done had he lived?"

"Yes, Henry, I would."

Lenny Sansone was bringing in Satan, and they turned toward him.

"That enough for him, Henry?" Lenny called.

Nodding, Henry turned back to Alec. "Let's get him, then," he said quietly.

"The Black? You mean it, Henry?" Alec asked anxiously.

"Sure. It's what you wanted, isn't it?" the trainer replied, moving off toward the sheds.

They were walking down the row when Jim Neville, the sports columnist, joined them. "Just got in this morning," he said. "What's this talk I hear about the Black not racing in the International, Henry?"

"He's been giving us trouble. We're not sure yet," Henry replied, continuing down the row.

"You mean there's some truth to this talk of Alec's not being able to handle him?" Jim asked.

The trainer was silent, so Jim turned to Alec. "What do you think, Alec?"

"I don't know either. If I can't control him, we'll withdraw him, Jim. No good could come of it if we raced him."

"When will you decide?" Jim asked.

"Within a few minutes," Henry said. "Stick around."

They were nearing the Black when they saw the crowd gathered in front of El Dorado's stall. Joining the group, they saw the track veterinarian in the stall with the golden stallion.

Alec overheard a man tell Henry, "El Dorado ran a high fever again last night, and they thought it best to get the vet."

Going to the stall door, Alec saw the veterinarian standing beside the stallion. El Dorado's head hung low and he constantly shifted his weight from one leg to another.

After a few minutes the veterinarian left the stall and hurried away. The group remained there for a while, then broke up, with Henry and Alec walking to the Black's stall.

"What do you think is wrong with El Dorado, Henry?" Alec asked.

The trainer's face was thoughtful, and he neither turned to the boy nor answered his question. Instead, he said, "Open the top of his door while I get the tack, Alec."

When Alec opened the door, the Black pushed his head toward him. Then the stallion caught sight of Avenger and Cavaliere coming in from the track, and he uttered his shrill scream. Moving inside the stall with him, Alec ran his hands down the long neck. "We're going out," he said. "And you've got to take it easy out there, Black. You've got to . . . or we go home."

Henry handed Alec the saddle, which the boy put on the Black. The stallion moved uneasily when Alec tightened the girth; then the boy took the bridle from Henry and slipped it over the stallion's head.

"He knows what's up, all right," Alec told Henry.

The Black pushed heavily against the door, his ears pricked and eyes gleaming. Kashmir went up the row toward the track, and the Black's gaze followed him as he screamed his challenge at the sorrel stallion.

"All right, Henry," Alec said. "Everything is okay."

Henry turned to see all the other people in the area watching them; then, taking the Black by the bridle, he opened the door.

With Alec holding him, the stallion moved quickly from the stall. He snorted repeatedly, but made no effort to rear or break away.

"I think he's going to do all right, Henry," Alec said.

"We've only just started," Henry returned.

The Black moved quickly up the row, as though eager to reach the track. Near the gate, Henry boosted Alec into the saddle. "What'd I tell you!" Alec said excitedly. "Not one bad move!"

Shaking his head, Henry said, "Sure seems you're right, Alec. Hard to believe. Get going now, but just a slow gallop."

It was only when the Black and Alec were on the track that Henry shouted. For the trainer's gaze had turned to Kashmir rounding the first turn and, suddenly, he thought he knew why the Black's head had turned neither to the left nor right coming up the row . . . why he had been so eager to reach the track. The Black knew Kashmir was ahead of him. He could be going after the sorrel stallion!

Henry shouted again to Alec, but the boy was out of hearing distance. Fearfully Henry watched the Black quickly shift his action to a full gallop. He saw Alec's attempts to hold him back, but there was no shortening of the giant strides. Surely the Black intended to run Kashmir down! Turning abruptly, Henry hurried back to the stables.

Alec kept a tight hold on the Black, remembering that Henry had told him he wanted only a slow gallop. But the Black had hold of the bit and was pulling hard. He wanted to stretch out still more. And it was only natural that he wanted to go, Alec thought, with Kashmir ahead of him.

Moving lower against the black neck, he called to his horse, "Take it easy, fella. It's too early. It's not the way Henry wants us to do it."

Still pulling, the Black moved into the first turn, and his strides lengthened even more.

When they came off the turn, Alec saw the sorrel stallion halfway down the backstretch. It was then that the Black screamed and took over. His body leveled out, yet his head was high with ears pricked forward.

There was nothing Alec could do now but stay with the Black. He had no control over him, for the stallion was running wild. Screaming, the Black bore down upon Kashmir and was directly behind him going into the turn.

The jockey riding Kashmir turned his head, then raised his whip to ward off the oncoming stallion. The Black lunged for Kashmir's neck. Desperately Alec tried to take him away as the whip came down to strike his horse on the nose. The blow caused the Black to miss his mark, and the stallion swerved abruptly, almost unseating Alec.

A moment later both stallions had come to a stop and were turning upon each other. Kashmir's jockey slid down from his horse. Alec fought the Black, trying to get him away. But the stallion rose to meet Kashmir. As Alec went up with him, he saw Henry and the other men, pitchforks and shovels in their hands, move in on the two fighting stallions.

The sorrel veered away at sight of the men and they caught him. When the Black came down, he bucked hard and Alec was thrown to the ground. For a moment he thought he was going to lose consciousness. When his vision cleared, there were many men holding on to the Black's bridle and they had a rope about his neck.

Alec knew that it was all over now, for this was the Black's answer. There would be no International Cup race for him.

An hour later, Alec stood quietly beside the Black in the closed stall. They were alone, for Henry had gone to the Race Secretary's office to withdraw the Black's name from the entries in the International Cup race.

Alec stood in the corner of the stall, waiting for the Black to come to him. He wanted desperately to make amends for bringing him here where he wasn't meant to be. He accepted the blame for all that had happened. Henry had warned him, but he had gone his way, believing he could control the Black despite the stallion's natural instinct to fight.

But all that was behind him now. He would start over again. He'd take the Black to the farm. Dad would meet him there, and they'd go ahead with their original plans while Henry raced Satan. Alec didn't even want to see the running of the International Cup. He'd stay at the farm with the Black.

"I know I've got a lot to make up for," he told the stallion. "None of it was your fault. You only did what your

natural instinct drove you to do. You haven't been trained
like the others. And in many ways I'm glad. I want you the
way you are, and that's why we're going away."

He had stood there a long while before the Black moved
in his direction. But the stallion stopped a few feet away and
without moving closer stretched his head to him. Alec let
him nuzzle his pocket, seeking the carrot that was there. He
raised his hand to the Black's nose, but the stallion pulled
back at his touch. Alec held the carrot out to him. The stallion extended his head again, and as Alec fed it to him he
succeeded in gently touching the soft nose.

For a long while he remained beside the Black before leaving the stall. Outside he saw the group gathered again in
front of El Dorado's stall. It seemed that everyone was there,
including the press. He was walking over when Henry
moved away from the group and came toward him.

"Is he any worse?" Alec asked when Henry reached him.

The trainer took him by the arm, turning him back toward the Black's stall. But Alec had had a chance to see the
worried and drawn looks on the faces of the men before El
Dorado's stall.

"I didn't get to the Race Secretary's office," Henry said
grimly. "I didn't need to."

"Why? What's the matter?" Henry still hadn't turned to
him, and Alec could catch only a glimpse of his face as they
walked along. And he didn't like what he saw there.

"The Race Secretary is over there," Henry said, "along
with the track vet and the State vet, who was called in."

"But why, Henry? Is El Dorado that sick?" Alec looked at
the crowd, now gathered in small, tight groups.

"It's serious, Alec," Henry said solemnly, turning to the

boy for the first time. "El Dorado has swamp fever, the most dreaded horse disease known. They're putting him down tonight," he added quietly. "There's no cure. . . . It's the only thing they can do."

The blood had left Alec's face, and it was only after a few minutes had passed that he asked hopefully, "But it's not contagious, is it, Henry?"

The trainer nodded without meeting the boy's eyes. "It is, Alec," he said. "It can reach epidemic proportions if not controlled. We can't leave. Every horse here has been placed in quarantine. A meeting has been called for tomorrow morning in the Secretary's office. We'll know more then."

Alec said nothing. Across the row were Avenger and Cavaliere and Kashmir, all with their heads pushed over their stall doors. Down the line on Alec's side were Phar Fly and Satan and Sea King . . . and just behind him was the Black. All of them had been exposed to swamp fever. There was no running away now. It was too late for that.

The Black whinnied, but Alec didn't turn to him. Instead he clasped his face in his hands, while Henry's arm went around his shoulders to steady him.

The Silent Killer

13

Their faces grave, the trainers filed into the office of the Race Secretary. Silently they took their seats around the long rectangular table at the head of which sat the Secretary. On his right was the State Veterinarian, and to the rear of the table were the sportswriters with their pads and pencils already in hand.

Alec sat beside Henry, waiting like everyone else.

The Secretary rose to his feet, and his eyes were on the sheet of paper lying on the table before him as he said, "The autopsy performed this morning on El Dorado proved without doubt that he had equine infectious anemia, commonly called swamp fever." He paused, his eyes leaving the paper for the men seated at the table. "I know that all of you have some knowledge of this disease, but at an earlier meeting this morning of the directors of the track and veterinarians we decided that it would be best for the State Veterinarian,

Doctor Murray, to acquaint you with all the facts concerning swamp fever. Doctor Murray," he announced, turning to the man on his right.

The State Veterinarian rose from his chair, his bald head directly in a beam of sunlight that found its way through the curtained window. "The cause of swamp fever," he said solemnly, "is a virus carried in the bloodstream. It is most commonly found in horses and mules. A horse may die of the first attack or, as is usually the case, he recovers and seems perfectly well until he experiences another attack. When the attacks come frequently, death follows shortly thereafter. Horses having swamp fever should be destroyed at once, so as not to infect healthy horses with the disease." Pausing, he added, "At present, there is no vaccine or immunity known to prevent a horse from contracting swamp fever."

The veterinarian was a tall man and now he straightened to his full height as he looked around the table. "The disease can reach epidemic proportions if not controlled. It is transmitted from infected horses to healthy animals by flies and mosquitoes or through stable equipment such as combs, brushes, saddles, bridles, blankets, and anything else which may have touched an abrasion of the infected horse and is then used on a healthy animal. It may spread, too, when infected and healthy horses are fed and watered from the same buckets or are in any way placed in intimate contact with one another."

The State Veterinarian paused again for a moment, his gaze dropping to the table, then returning to the men who listened to him in sober silence.

"Your horses have all been exposed to this disease," he

continued very gravely. "Even now they may have it, for the incubation period of swamp fever is generally from seven to twenty-eight days, during which time there are no obvious characteristic symptoms. The symptoms, when they do appear, are a fever of one hundred five or as high as one hundred eight degrees Fahrenheit; dejection, usually with low-hanging head; a shifting of weight from one leg to another; breathing more quickly, sometimes with abdomen; swelling of legs and loss of weight.

"Your horses, gentlemen, are now under a sixty-day quarantine, the approximate time necessary for us to determine whether or not they are infected. It is regrettable, but this is the only possible action the state can take to prevent this fatal disease from spreading. The directors of the track have had no alternative but to cancel the International Cup race, and we're asking you gentlemen to take your horses to a state farm a short distance away, where screening tests will be made to ascertain whether or not any horse has contracted swamp fever from El Dorado. We cannot force you to move your horses to the farm or to take the tests, but I must remind you, gentlemen, that in all fairness to the hundreds of horses due to arrive shortly at this track for the regular meeting, you owe it to them and to the sport in general to remove your horses to the farm, so that there will be no opportunity for this disease to spread any further."

The State Veterinarian paused for a long while, then said, "Gentlemen, I would like a show of hands of those who will consent to move their horses to the farm."

Despondently all the men raised their hands. No questions were asked. No word was spoken. The cancellation of the race to which they had looked forward for so many months was of no importance now to any one of them. Instead, each was haunted by the fear that his horse might be stricken . . . that before long he, too, would have to consent to the destruction of his horse. They were the trainers of the world's finest horses . . . horses that in the years to come were to have passed on their speed to their get for the improvement of the breed. Now, they were to be exiled.

The State Veterinarian was speaking again, and the men raised their eyes to his. "Your horses can have swamp fever without showing the characteristic symptoms," he said. "The only definite way we have of finding out is to take blood samples from your horses and, pooling this blood, inoculate it into the bloodstream of a horse who has not been exposed to the disease. If no evidence of the disease appears in the inoculated test horse, your horses will be given a clean bill of health and released. However, if swamp fever develops in the test horse, each of your horses must be tested individually to find out which one or more has the disease."

The State Veterinarian cleared his throat. "I know the difficult time that is ahead of you, gentlemen. We appreciate the full cooperation you have promised us. We hope, as you do, that none of your horses will be found to have swamp fever and that clean bills of health will be given to all. We request that you have your horses ready to leave the track by noon. All horses will travel individually, and we'll have vans for those of you who don't have any here."

They filed out as quietly as they had entered the office, while behind them the press gathered around the Race Secretary and the State Veterinarian.

Outside the building Alec and Henry walked slowly, neither saying a word for a long while.

"We'd better call your father," Henry said finally. "He

ought to hear about it from us instead of the newspapers."

"It's all over, isn't it, Henry?" Alec asked. "Everything we'd planned."

"Don't be silly, Alec," Henry said a little angrily. "Maybe none of the horses have it . . . just like the doc said. We have to make sure, that's all. El Dorado couldn't have had swamp fever very long, and the chances are good that it never had a chance to spread. There isn't a stable in the row which hasn't been sprayed daily with DDT, as we've been doin'. I've hardly seen a fly around here, much less a mosquito. An' don't forget none of us ever used any of El Dorado's stable equipment," he added assuredly. "We all minded our own business and that's what counts right now . . . no contact with El Dorado."

"There's just one thing," Alec began slowly, then stopped.

"What thing?" Henry asked.

"The day after El Dorado arrived . . . it was when you went to pick up Satan at the airport."

"Yeah," Henry said impatiently, then hesitated. "What about it?"

"I loaned one of our buckets to the fellow who took care of him."

Henry halted in his tracks. "But he didn't give it back to you, did he?"

"He did, Henry . . . that same afternoon."

Proceeding again, Henry said with feigned lightness, "I don't think it matters, Alec. There's very little chance . . ."

"But I don't like to think of that . . . even a little chance."

"You been usin' the bucket? You remember which one it was?"

They turned down Row C. "Yes, Henry, I've been using it

to water the Black." Alec's face was twisted in his anxiety.

"I'm sure nothin' will come of it," Henry said. "The contact with the infected horse has to be more intimate than that to catch swamp fever."

"But the vet said they shouldn't be watered from the same buckets," Alec returned insistently.

"He probably meant at the same time," Henry replied. "No sense worryin' about it now, Alec. Let's get rid of the bucket and forget it. The Black has shown no symptoms of swamp fever and all that was a couple of weeks ago."

"The vet said some horses don't show any symptoms at all."

"Cut it out, Alec," Henry said angrily. "You're not makin' it any easier for yourself or for me. Why jump ahead looking for trouble? We can't do anything now but wait."

When they reached the stall Alec went to the stallion, while Henry said, "I'll get Satan ready first."

"I'll be with you in a minute," Alec said quietly.

The Black nuzzled his fingers. Tears came to the boy's eyes while he looked at the stallion. He started to say something to him, but found he couldn't talk. Turning away, he saw Satan's head pushed over his stall door. The Black nipped playfully at Alec's shirt for attention. But just now he couldn't look at either of his horses.

Exiled!

14

It was a little after noon when the vans left the International track. As they went through the barn gate, turning onto the highway, Henry said to Alec, "A racetrack named for a race that never was run . . . that's ironical." Shrugging his shoulders, he added, "But maybe next year it'll come off. At least, that's what they're planning."

"Maybe it will," Alec muttered. "But how many of these horses will be around to be in it?"

"There you go again," Henry replied sullenly. "Cut it out, Alec."

"I'm sorry, Henry."

Closely following the car driven by the State Veterinarian, the seven vans carrying Satan, the Black, Sea King, Avenger, Phar Fly, Kashmir and Cavaliere went through town. People lined the streets, watching the procession with sober but curious faces.

Henry grimaced as he looked at the people. "You'd think it was a funeral procession," he said angrily. "Why, you'd think . . ." he stopped, turning to Alec. "We're just making sure," he added emphatically. "The vet said the chances are all in our favor that none of the horses contracted swamp fever from El Dorado."

"I know," Alec said quietly. "That's what you said before, Henry."

Their gazes met, and Henry was the first to turn away. "I told you your dad was driving up to join us, didn't I?" he asked, quickly changing the subject.

"Yes, you did."

"He was leaving right away," Henry continued. "So I told him to meet us at the inn in Mountainview . . . that's the town near the state farm. At least, that's what they told me in the office."

They had left the track far behind and were now going northwest on a highway which stretched toward a vivid panorama of woods and mountains. The van directly ahead of them carried Satan; it had been provided, together with a driver, by the Race Secretary. His eyes upon the van, Alec asked, "How did Lenny and Fred take your sending them back to the city?"

"'They wanted to see it through, but what could they do?" Henry asked. "You and I can handle Satan an' the Black while they're here. No sense in payin' wages when there's no work to be done. Lenny can pick up some mounts at the Belmont meeting, an' there's work for Fred there, too. Both of 'em can use the money, so there's no sense in their just waitin' around."

They drove for many miles in silence, then Alec asked,

"This blood test they're going to take at the farm, Henry. Do you understand exactly what they're going to do?"

"I've got a pretty good idea, Alec. From what the vet said, they intend to take blood samples from each racer; then they'll pool the blood and put this combined sample into a healthy horse . . . one the vet will get."

Alec shook his head. "Poor devil," he said. "He's the guinea pig. . . . Then we all just watch him to see if he comes down with swamp fever."

"An' if he doesn't," Henry said, "we know that none of the racers have swamp fever."

"But if he does?" Alec asked.

"Then the vet knows someone's got it," Henry said grimly. "The whole business is repeated then, only this time the vet will probably bring in seven test horses—one for each of the racers. They'll be tested individually until the vet has isolated the one . . . or maybe more . . . of the racers who's carrying the disease."

"But the blood test won't be necessary for any horse that definitely shows any symptoms of the disease, as El Dorado did. Is that it, Henry?"

"Yes, that's it. There wouldn't be any reason for givin' that horse the blood test, Alec. They'd know right away that he had swamp fever and he would have to be destroyed." Henry paused. "But none of the racers have shown any symptoms yet . . . and I don't think they're going to."

Alec was silent for a long while before asking, "How long will the blood test take, Henry?"

"They say at least forty days. So we'll be here for quite a spell. The incubation period of swamp fever can be as long as twenty-eight days, the vet said; then they'll wait maybe another two weeks for any symptoms to show up in the test horse."

Two hours later they crossed the great open fields of a valley and entered the small village of Mountainview. Far to the north were wind-swept peaks, barren and jagged against the sky. But just to the west, and behind the village, was a low mountain range . . . a forest of spruce, pine and hemlock.

The only two-story building in the village was the inn, which Alec and Henry passed without stopping. They turned sharp left a short distance farther on, going onto a blacktop road that went toward the wooded mountain range. They drove for a mile across the open plain, then crossed a bridge over a wide river, and continued on toward the range. The paved road ended a mile farther on, becoming dirt as it squeezed its way through the heavily wooded region.

"They're certainly getting us away from everything," Alec said, looking at the dense forest on either side of the van.

But the road continued to be level and smooth, and they were able to make good time. A mile and a half from where they had entered the woods the road veered to the left and wound up a slight incline. A short distance farther on, the trees gave way to a large tract of cleared land.

The road came in at the upper end of the clearing, and directly ahead of them was a long white barn. Behind the barn was a small fenced pasture, going back to meet the woods and a sharp rise in the ground. A stone house was there, nestled amid the pines. The rest of the clearing lay to the left of the road and it, too, was fenced for pasture; at this end it was widest, gradually narrowing as it found its way through the forest only to be lost from sight by a sharp curve a few hundred yards away.

The State Veterinarian stopped his car just past the barn doors and got out to talk to a man who met him. Finally he turned to the vans, waving them on to the barn.

Henry drove to the front of the barn and parked alongside the van occupied by Satan. "C'mon, Alec," he said.

They got out and stood in front of their van, awaiting instructions from the veterinarian, while the other vans were parked. Behind the van came the cars carrying the newspapermen.

Henry said impatiently, "I'll get the vet to let us put the Black in the barn first, Alec. Get him ready."

When Henry left, Alec let down the back door of the van and went inside. The stallion neighed, and Alec said, "We're getting off now, boy."

He had untied the Black when Henry reappeared at the back of the van. "Okay, Alec," the trainer said. "They're ready for him."

Alec turned the stallion carefully, talking to him all the while. The Black stopped at the ramp, his eyes shifting to the long field opposite the barn doors. One of the other stallions neighed; the Black's ears pitched forward and he whistled.

When Alec stepped onto the ramp the stallion followed him down and onto the ground with no hesitation. The Black moved quickly about and his gaze turned again to the field; the gate was open, but the stallion made no attempt to pull away from Alec when the boy led him toward the barn.

"Take him all the way down to the end stall on your left," the veterinarian told Alec when the boy reached him; then, turning to Henry, he added, "Put Satan two stalls up from him, Mr. Dailey, if you will. We're keeping an empty stall between the horses, but all of them are to go on this one side of the barn."

Alec walked the Black down the long corridor, and the stallion's hoofs beat rhythmically on the wooden flooring. The box stalls were high and closed above with a heavy wire screen. The stallion stopped before his stall, but Alec turned him in a circle, then led him inside.

As he shut the door behind them Satan entered the barn, walking beside Henry. The burly black colt swept his ears back when the Black screamed at him. Satan moved restlessly, but continued following Henry. Alec was going to him when Henry said, "Better stay away, Alec. The Black won't like it any."

Henry had Satan in his stall when Phar Fly entered the barn, followed closely by Avenger, Cavaliere, Sea King and Kashmir.

When they were all inside their stalls the Black was still screaming his challenging blasts. And his eyes blazed fiercely through the wire mesh as he looked up the row at the other stallions.

"He ought to get used to having them around, now," Henry said. "He's not going to have anything else to look at for a long while."

"What difference does it make now?" Alec asked bitterly.

But Henry didn't answer.

Jim Neville left the group of reporters gathered about the State Veterinarian and walked over to them. "I'm sorry," he told Alec. "I feel partly responsible for the Black's being here. I haven't forgotten the talk we had, Alec."

"It was my decision to make," Alec said, walking away.

"I'm the only one responsible for anything that happens."

The boy went outside the barn, his eyes following the white fence of the field beyond, noting that it extended all along the edges of the forest. "They won't even be able to get out there," he said bitterly. "They can't even eat off the same ground."

He had been standing there many minutes when a small coupe came down the road. He watched it as it drew closer. Then suddenly he burst into a run.

His father sat behind the wheel of the car, and beside him was Tony!

Reaching the car, Alec jumped into it, and his father's hand clasped his arm. "We got to the inn early and found out how to get here," Mr. Ramsay said.

Tony was first out of the car. "I come when your father tell me this-a terrible thing, Aleec," he said sadly. "I no can work, so I come."

"It was good of you, Tony," Alec said. Then, nodding toward the barn, he added, "They're all in there . . . Henry, too."

"You coming?" his father asked, when he and Tony started for the barn without Alec.

"I think I'll stay here, Dad. Henry will tell you everything we know."

Alec walked up the road and didn't return to the barn until he saw the State Veterinarian appear at the door, with the trainers gathered about him. He reached them in time to hear the veterinarian say, "The test horse will be here to-morrow, and we have decided to take blood samples of your horses then. After the inoculation of the test horse, there won't be anything to do but wait. You can feel free to leave your horses in our care, well knowing that everything possible will be done for them. Or you can stay . . . whichever suits your plans better. If no evidence of swamp fever is disclosed in the test horse, clean bills of health will be given your horses in forty days. I would like to ask that you leave with me your forwarding address if you decide to leave Mountainview. We would, of course, have to get in touch with you immediately if swamp fever developed in your horse."

The State Veterinarian turned to his assistants, and it was obvious to all that the meeting was over. Taking Alec by the arm, Henry said, "Let's get our stuff out of the vans and put it in the stall between Satan and the Black; then we'll feed 'em and have just enough time to get back to the inn before dark."

"Can't we stay here, Henry?"

"No, they don't want us sleeping in the barn. Besides, we'll do better at the inn nights. We'll be needin' our rest with forty long days ahead of us."

"I only hope it's forty days," Alec said. "I wouldn't want anything to happen sooner."

Mr. Ramsay went along with them to help unload their tack. But Tony, unnoticed by the others, stayed behind, and as soon as the huckster saw them enter Henry's van he moved closer to the veterinarian. Patiently he waited until the veterinarian moved away from his assistants and headed for the stone house. Tony followed him.

"Meester Veterinary," he called. "One minute, please." And when the veterinarian stopped and turned to him, Tony said, "I am good friend of Aleec Ramsay and Henree Dailey."

The veterinarian smiled. "I'm sure you are," he said. "What can I do for you?"

"My horse, Napoleon, he's-a good friend of the Black and Satan." Tony paused to look over his shoulder. "Maybe it would be better if I walk with you to your house, yes? It is something very private I wish to say to you."

Tony waited until they had reached the wide veranda of the house before continuing. "This-a test horse I hear you and my friend Henree talk about. In him you will put the blood of the Black and Satan, yes?"

"Yes," the veterinarian said. "Their blood along with samples from others will be inoculated into the test horse."

"You have this-a test horse?"

"He will be here tomorrow."

"You could use maybe another one, too? One to take the blood of Satan and the Black?"

The veterinarian's gaze met Tony's. "You mean your horse?"

"He one healthy horse, my Nappy," Tony said excitedly. "He never sick in his life."

"But I have a test horse, and one is all we need now."

"But it's-a better if you have two, yes?" Tony insisted. "If Napoleon no get sick, you know what you look for is in five horses, not seven. Five is smaller than seven, yes?"

"Naturally, the smaller the group the better," the veterinarian said. "If Napoleon developed swamp fever and the other test horse didn't, we'd know Satan or the Black—or possibly both of them—was the carrier of the disease."

"Then you will use him," Tony said. "You make me one happy man, Meester Veterinary."

The veterinarian watched Tony closely. "You're sure you

want to do this? We could get along without your Napoleon now, and if by chance he should contract swamp fever from the inoculation it means certain death, you know."

"My Nappy . . . I'm sure he wants it this-a way," Tony said more soberly. "He's-a like brother to the Black and Satan. And now he will have their blood in him. It's the only way, Meester Veterinary."

"All right," the veterinarian said quietly. "It will make our job easier. When can you have him here?"

"Tomorrow morning I be back," Tony said excitedly. "I go now and get him, and we drive all night." Turning, Tony ran hard to Henry's van.

He took one look in the back of the van to make sure all the tack had been removed, then slammed the door shut and went to the front. Inside the cab, he turned on the ignition and started the motor. He had the van in gear and was slowly moving away when Henry, Alec and Mr. Ramsay appeared at the barn door.

It was only when Tony had the van in high gear and was speeding down the road that he waved to them.

"Now what's come over him?" Henry asked. "And where's he going with my van?"

"Probably back to the inn," Mr. Ramsay suggested. "But I don't understand why he didn't wait for us."

"I can't see it either," Alec said; then he looked over at the stone house, to find the veterinarian standing on the porch, watching the van until it had disappeared among the trees. "I wonder," he muttered.

"Wonder what, Alec?" Henry asked.

"Nothing, Henry. Nothing."

Small, Worried World

15

Early the following morning, Alec, Henry and Mr. Ramsay left their rooms at the inn and went to the small dining room for breakfast. Already the room was crowded with trainers, owners and reporters, but Henry was able to find three empty seats at the counter.

"I still can't understand Tony's fadeout," he said as they sat down.

"He probably wanted to get back to work," Mr. Ramsay said, after they had given their orders. "But he did tell me he had arranged for a friend to take over his route while he was away. I was under the impression that he intended to stay here awhile. He was so concerned about the Black and Satan."

"But why did he have to take my van?" Henry persisted. " 'Course I don't have any use for it just now. But he could have asked me, anyway. I don't like it."

"No," Mr. Ramsay agreed, "and I don't blame you. It's not at all like Tony." Turning to Alec, he asked, "What do you think is the reason for his leaving, Alec?"

The boy shrugged his shoulders. "Tony usually has a good reason for anything he does. So I'm just letting it go at that. I'm sure we'll know before long."

"We'd better," Henry growled, turning to the plate of ham and eggs which the counterman had placed before him.

When they had finished breakfast and were leaving, Henry stopped to talk to the other trainers before rejoining Alec and Mr. Ramsay outside the inn.

"Seems like 'most everybody is leavin'," Henry said as they got into Mr. Ramsay's car. "They don't see what good their hanging around is goin' to do. If the worst comes, they'll hear of it soon enough. I guess they're right. The vet and his assistants are takin' over completely."

"Still, I want to stick around," Alec said as Mr. Ramsay started the car and drove down the street.

"With us it's different," Henry returned. "The vet and his boys can handle Satan all right, but not the Black. We'll have to take care of him ourselves."

Mr. Ramsay turned the car down the blacktop road and started across the open fields. They had reached the bridge when he said, "And that's not the only reason it's different for us, Henry. The others have more horses, if anything should happen to those here. But we don't. Satan and the Black are all we have . . . and upon them we have built all our hopes for the future. We have nothing if we lose them."

Henry glanced at Alec, to find the boy's gaze directly on the road ahead. "Yes," the trainer admitted, turning to Mr. Ramsay, "you're right, of course. But nothin' is goin' to happen to either one of 'em. Or to any of the others. I'd wager almost anything that none of the horses here will come down with swamp fever. The chances are good that they'd be showing some symptoms by now if they'd picked up the disease from El Dorado. But none of 'em show a thing yet . . . an' I don't think they will."

Coming off the bridge, they continued across the fields until they reached the dirt road. The woods closed in on them, shutting out the morning sun. After going a mile and a half, they came to the sharp left turn and went up the slight incline to the farm.

There was but one van parked in front of the barn, and they looked at it with incredulous eyes.

"Henry!" Alec shouted. "It's yours!"

"It sure is!" Henry returned. "It's mine all right. But why did Tony . . ."

"Look! In the pasture, Henry!" Alec cried.

Then they all saw the gray, sway-backed figure of Napoleon as the horse grazed contentedly in the field.

"But why would Tony get Napoleon?" Mr. Ramsay asked. "I don't get it at all, Henry." He brought the car to a stop before the barn. "Not at all," he repeated.

"I'm beginning to," Henry said slowly.

"I had a hunch this might be it," Alec said, getting out of the car. "But I still didn't believe I could be right."

Napoleon raised his heavy head, neighing to them before once more turning to the grass.

"What are you two driving at?" Mr. Ramsay asked.

"We think Tony had his own idea as to who should be the test horse," Henry said, leading the way toward the barn. "But let's find out for sure."

Entering the barn, they found the veterinarian and his assistants, all dressed in long white cloaks, leaving Satan's stall. And Tony was with them.

Alec and Henry ran forward, and when they reached the group, the veterinarian said, "I'm glad you're here. Tony said it would be wiser to have you around with him." He nodded toward the Black. "We have taken blood samples from all except him."

Henry and Alec glanced at Tony, who sheepishly moved away from the stall door.

"I'll stay at his head," Alec said. "I don't think it'll be easy working around him."

"It'll only take a minute," the veterinarian returned.

"Put the lead shank on him and pass it through to me in the next stall," Henry suggested, handing the shank to Alec. "It'll be easier holdin' him that way."

Before going inside the stall, Alec got a container of oats and a pocketful of carrots. The Black came to him when the boy poured the oats into the corner feedbox. Snapping the lead shank onto his halter, Alec passed the end through the wire screen to Henry in the next stall.

The boy stood close to the stallion's head, fondling him while he ate the grain. But the Black stopped eating as soon as the veterinarian and his assistants entered the stall. He pulled back, only to find himself held close by the shank and Alec's hand on his halter. His hindquarters shifted quickly, but the men were close to his neck before his hindlegs flew out, striking the side of the stall. The men stood still then, waiting while Alec talked to the stallion and offered him a handful of oats. Finally the Black took the oats from Alec, but his eyes constantly shifted to the strangers in his stall.

Patiently the veterinarian waited until the stallion turned from Alec's hand to the feedbox. But he stopped eating again when he felt their hands upon his neck. He jerked his head up, but the shank held him close. He swung his hindquarters once more, attempting to pin the men against the wall, then moved quickly away from them when he came up against the pointed stick an assistant held in his hand for just such an emergency.

"I guess we'll have to use the rail to keep him still," the veterinarian said finally.

One of the men left the stall to return a few minutes later with a long wooden bar, which he shoved through the door and put to one side of the Black to keep his hindquarters from shifting.

The stallion moved against it, but the bar stopped him from going any farther. Alec stayed at his head, talking to him, offering him carrots and grain.

"They're not going to hurt you," he said. "It'll be over in a matter of seconds. They've got to do it. It's not going to hurt."

The veterinarian and his assistants were outside the bar. Alec saw the needle and knew they were going to work. The stallion pushed heavily against the bar, but it didn't give way. Instead it held him close to the side of his stall. He tried jerking his head back again, but the lead shank held him still. He could fight now, but there wouldn't be any getting away.

The Black made two more futile efforts to free himself, while Alec stood by his head, helpless to do anything to make it easier for his horse. He could not see the veterinarian, nor did he want to. He continued rubbing the Black's head and at the same time offering him the carrots, which went unnoticed.

Suddenly the Black threw back his head, almost breaking the lead shank. Alec's hand went to the halter. As he held him, he realized that the stallion had felt the sharp prick of the needle. But that would be all there was to it. It was over now.

A moment later the veterinarian straightened with the vial of the Black's blood in his hand. He left the stall and the others with him followed after the bar had been removed.

Unsnapping the lead shank, Alec waited while the stallion moved restlessly about his stall, his gaze following the men as they walked down the corridor. It was only when they were out of sight that he turned to his feedbox and Alec.

While the stallion ate, Alec remained with him.

Outside the stall Henry and Mr. Ramsay were talking to Tony, and Alec could overhear their conversation without leaving the stall.

"He say it is okay with him for Nappy to be test horse for Satan and the Black," Tony was explaining. "So I go an get him. It is the way it should be. You understand, Henree, yes?"

"Sure, I guess I do," Henry replied. "Then I guess they're pooling the blood of the other horses and are goin' to put it in the vet's test horse. Is that it, Tony?"

"Already they do that," Tony said excitedly. "Before you come they do that. He's in the pasture behind the barn. They kept him away from Nappy. They take no chances for anything, the veterinary say." Tony's hands were on the arms of Henry and Mr. Ramsay. "But now they put the blood of Satan and the Black in my Nappy. You come and see, yes?

It's-a big moment for Nappy. Now he will be real brother to Satan and the Black. It's-a one moment we never forget. . . ."

Alec left the Black, following the others until he came to Satan's stall. The colt had his long nose stretched out, and Alec's hand went to him. But the boy's gaze remained upon the back of the little huckster as he said, "I know we won't forget it, Tony. And I only hope everything turns out all right . . . for you and Napoleon as well as for Satan and the Black . . . and for us."

From the moment that Napoleon was inoculated with the blood samples from Satan and the Black, Alec slipped into his own small and worried world. Day after day he spent alone, talking little to his father and Henry and always watching fearfully for the dreaded symptoms of swamp fever.

When the first week passed with no change in the condition of the racers Henry said, "See, Alec, just like I figured. It's been long enough now since they were exposed to El Dorado for them to show some symptoms, if they had it. Now all we've got to do is watch the test horses, an' if nothing happens to either of 'em we're sure all the racers are free of swamp fever."

But Alec did not share Henry's optimism. He didn't want to build up any false hopes. The racers still could be carriers of the disease, and pass it on to Napoleon or the other test horse. It was too early to tell with them. The incubation period of swamp fever, the veterinarian had said, was from seven to twenty-eight days. And just to be very certain they were going to wait forty days from the time of inoculation. Forty days! And it was only a little over a week since the blood had passed from the racers to the test horses. It was too early to tell . . . much too early to share anyone's optimism, even Henry's. So Alec withdrew into his world again, and each passing day seemed a lifetime.

Mr. Ramsay stayed with them, and Tony left only occasionally on short visits to the city to make certain his customers were being served. "This-a boy who has taken over my route is a good friend," he told them. "But maybe once in a while he needs me, so I go to him. No, I'm no worried about my Nappy getting this-a swamp fever. He no get anything but good blood from Satan and the Black. He's happy here, yes? Just eat grass all day long. He work hard all his life, so now he take it easy. That's-a good . . . very good. An' now he's-a famous, too. . . . Everyone knows my Nappy. . . . That's-a good, too."

Napoleon's picture appeared in the newspapers regularly, for the two test horses had become international figures. The world knew that the fate of Avenger, Cavaliere, Kashmir, Phar Fly, Sea King, Satan and the Black depended upon the state of health of these two horses. So each day their condition was reported by press services to the far corners of the world. And the daily message was repeated, "No change in test horses on fourteenth day." . . . "No change on fifteenth day." . . . "No change on eighteenth day."

The third week passed and with it Henry's optimism rose to greater heights. "Come on, Alec," he kidded. "Crack a smile. Everything is goin' to be okay. Why, even the vet says the chances are getting better with every day now. If Napoleon or the other test horse had contracted swamp fever from their inoculations they'd be showing some signs of it. But they're in better health than they ever were. Napoleon's actin' like a colt. See for yourself!"

Alec watched the old gray as he galloped and rolled luxuriously in the tall grass. "But I want to be sure, Henry," he said, ". . . so sure, before I let go. And I won't be until it's all over, and I have clean bills of health for Satan and the Black in my hand."

The last of September came, bringing rich and colorful fall dress to many of the trees. But the days remained unseasonably hot, and there was no sign of rain to break the prolonged dry spell that had existed since their arrival at the state farm. There were reports of small forest fires being fought to the north and west. And such talk didn't lessen Alec's anxiety while going through each day at the farm.

Napoleon remained in the field, although much of the grass had been burned out by the hot sun, and hay was being fed him for a substitute. Alec spent part of each day with the old gray, watching him more closely perhaps than anyone else for any symptoms of swamp fever. But Napoleon remained active, and Alec would follow him as he sought green blades of grass along the wooded edges of the long and narrow field. It was on one of these days that the boy came upon a barred gate, half-hidden by creeping vines. He stood there for a moment, looking down the forest lane on the other side of the gate and wondering where it led. Perhaps it joined the road leading to the valley. Perhaps not. It could have a dead end, just going to another clearing or farm building. But it wasn't important, and he left the gate to follow Napoleon around the bend in the field to the lower pasture in the gray's search of grass untouched by the sun.

With the coming of October, Henry's optimism rose to still greater heights. "Another two and a half weeks an' we'll be on our way to our farm," he told Alec. "We'll spend the winter there and put up separate pastures for the Black and Satan. It'll do 'em both a lot of good to be out most of the winter, if the weather is decent at all."

"And there's that school just a short distance away from the farm, Alec," his father said. "I've been corresponding with them and you'll be able to enroll even though you'll be a little late."

Eagerly Alec looked at them. "It sounds so good. I just . . ." He stopped, and the enthusiasm left his eyes. "It's still too early to start planning," he said. "We have seventeen days to go."

During the following week, the nights turned cold but the days remained warm, and still there was no sign of rain in the cloudless skies. Leaves dropped from trees, and if it hadn't been for the forest of evergreens the mountains would have stood bare and forlorn.

"I wish it would rain," Alec told Henry. "I don't like hearing all this talk of forest fires. That farm is a trap if anything happens around here."

"There you go borrowin' trouble again," Henry retorted. "Natives always talk that way this time of the year. The forest rangers know their job. You've got nothing to worry about."

Then came renewed activity in the village of Mountainview and at the state farm. For now that the test was coming quickly to its end, owners and trainers returned. Laughter and loud talk of races to be run the coming year were heard, and no longer were the faces of the men haggard with fear for the safety of their horses. Henry joined them in their discussions, but Alec stayed away, still counting off the remaining days as each went by.

The last day of the test arrived, and late in the afternoon the State Veterinarian called the owners, trainers and press to the porch of his home. In his hands were the certificates testifying to the good health of the racers stabled in the barn.

The veterinarian began by thanking the group for their cooperation and patience. But Alec wasn't listening to him; instead he was whispering excitedly in Henry's ear, "This is it, Henry! This is what I've been waiting for. Satan and the Black are . . ."

"Shh," Henry said.

But Alec went on, his enthusiasm and happiness knowing no bounds. "They're all right, Henry. Both of them. We can take them home. Let's try to buy a couple of good mares for the Black right this winter, Henry," he added quickly. "Then we can start breeding right away. Don't you think that's a good idea . . . to get going right now, I mean?"

Henry turned to him. "Sure, Alec," he whispered. "It's a good idea, providing we can find the right mares."

Henry's name was called by the veterinarian, and he went forward to get their two certificates.

A short while later the group broke up, with the veterinarian suggesting that they remove the horses from the farm the following morning, if possible.

They all went to the barn, where the news photographers were taking pictures. Napoleon was in the stall directly opposite the Black, and Tony was with him. Waving the certificate, Alec ran to the stall.

"He's-a part Black and part Satan now," Tony said with a grin, when Napoleon pushed his head hard against the boy. "See, Aleec, he knows it. But now he mus' go back to work and maybe he no like that."

"Tony," Alec said, "I've wanted to ask you something."
The huckster stopped fondling Napoleon. "Yes, Aleec?"

"You said that Napoleon has worked hard all his life, didn't you?"

"You betcha. I get him when he was three year old. An' now he's-a seventeen. That's," Tony stopped to count on his fingers, "fourteen years I work him."

"Would you want to retire him then?"

Tony looked at the boy, and slowly the small pinpoints of light in his black eyes flared brightly. "You mean, Aleec . . ."

"We'd sure like to have him at the farm, Tony. But he'd still be your horse. He could take it nice and easy for the rest of his life. He'd be a big help to us, too, Tony, for he gets along so well with both the Black and Satan. But how do you feel about it?"

"Sure, I mees him," Tony said. "But when you love a horse you think of him, yes? So I think of him and I say he go with you, Aleec . . . to rest and play."

"But you'll promise to come up to the farm every weekend, when Mother and Dad come up? You'll do that, Tony?"

"You no can keep me away, Aleec. I come to see you and Nappy every week. We go now?" he asked excitedly.

"No, not until tomorrow morning. But we'll get an early start and be at our farm before dark. And just think, Tony," he added slowly, "all this will be behind us."

"An' forgotten, yes?" Tony asked.

"Yes, forgotten," Alec repeated, rubbing Napoleon's nose, while behind him the Black neighed shrilly for attention.

Trapped!

16

Back at the inn that same evening, a party was held in the dining room. And now that the haunting fear of swamp fever was a thing of the past, each owner and trainer talked only of the speed of his horse . . . of Sea King and Kashmir, of Avenger and Phar Fly, of Cavaliere and Satan. For many hours they discussed the race that had never been run and what might have happened. And they talked about the possibility of their horses meeting this coming winter in Florida, or next summer, or perhaps not until next year's running of the International Cup.

"And maybe never," Alec heard Henry tell the group. "Things happen fast in this business. Who can tell what's goin' to happen even a few months from now? I'm not one for doin' my racing ahead of time."

"And what about the Black, Henry?" someone asked. "You must have some plans for him. He'll need some real schooling if you intend to race him."

"Alec is retiring him," Henry replied. "Satan is going to do the racing for this stable."

Jim Neville left the group and joined Alec. "They've all been talking a good race except you, Alec. What do you think about it?"

"The International, you mean?"

Jim nodded.

Shrugging his shoulders, Alec said, "What difference does it make now who would've won? I haven't even thought about it for a long time."

"For forty days?"

"Yes," Alec said, "for forty days." He paused before adding, "It wasn't important then, and it isn't now."

"You're right, of course," Jim said. "But now that the danger is over, it's only human nature for us to go back and try to guess what would have happened in a race of that kind."

"I wouldn't have been in it anyway," Alec said.

"You were actually going to withdraw the Black from the race?"

"Sure we were, Jim. You saw what happened with Kashmir. It isn't fair to the Black or to the others. He's not trained to race."

"But he could be," Jim suggested slowly.

"We've been through this before," Alec replied a little angrily. "I don't want it that way. You know that, Jim."

"I know," Jim agreed, trying to appease the boy. "I just thought you might have changed your mind."

"I'm more certain now than ever before," Alec said.

Henry joined them, and Jim Neville turned to him, asking, "You told me back at the track, Henry, that Satan wasn't going to have any trouble winning the International. I was wondering if that was before or after you and Alec had decided to withdraw the Black?"

Henry turned to Alec and found the boy's intent gaze upon him. Lowering his eyes, Henry said, "What difference does it make? They're both in our stable."

"None," Jim replied, "except I thought I'd just like to know. You remember saying that Satan was the faster."

"All right. It was before we decided to withdraw the Black," Henry interrupted. "But that was only my opinion." Henry met the boy's gaze. "And certainly not Alec's," he concluded.

Mr. Ramsay and Tony joined them, and Henry managed to change the subject.

After the party ended, Alec and Henry went out on the inn's porch. The night was clear and the strong wind felt good on their faces. Sitting down on the steps, Alec said, "We'll put Napoleon and the Black in your van won't we, Henry?"

"Yes," his friend said, sitting down beside him. "I've hired another van and driver to follow us with Satan. Tony will ride with your father, I guess."

"And we're still figuring on an early start?"

"The earlier the better," Henry replied. "It'll be wise to get the Black outa the barn before the others start leaving . . . means less excitement all around."

"It's going to be good to get away from all this," Alec said.

Henry smiled. "I don't mind all this talkin' that goes on

though, Alec. Fact is, I kinda like it. The older you get the more you seem to talk about what your horse could have done or what he might do. None of us means any harm by it. An' even the sportswriters—like Jim Neville—talk about it because it's their interest just like ours. An' the more they get us to talk the more stories they seem to get for their papers. An' that's the way it goes."

"I know," Alec said. "It's just that it's too soon after what . . ."

"You took it too hard for too long," Henry interrupted. "I told you to relax a couple of weeks ago."

"Sure you did," Alec said. "But I couldn't do it."

The lights had been turned out, and the sound of footsteps on the stairs had long since died away, when a car came down the street, stopping before the inn. A man got out, carrying a small suitcase.

Alec and Henry had moved to one side of the steps to give him room to pass.

" 'Evening," Henry said.

"Good evening," the man returned. He stopped, pointing to the north. "They got another forest fire up there. I passed it this afternoon on the way down the valley."

Turning to the north, Henry and Alec could just make out the red glow on the horizon. "How far north?" Henry asked anxiously.

"Oh, must be a hundred miles. We don't need to worry about that one," the man added assuredly. "They had it under control all right."

" 'That one'?" Henry repeated. "Are there any other fires?"

"Oh, no, I didn't mean that there *are* other fires. It's just that one never can tell with the woods so dry and no rain at all. It's sure bad . . . all along the line it's bad. Keeps the rangers busy, all right. But they have the equipment and never seem to let these fires get too far out of hand before they control them. Well, good night now."

When the man had left them, Henry said sarcastically, "A real cheerful guy."

"But I still don't like the idea of having a fire so close," Alec said. "This is the closest yet."

"A hundred miles isn't so close," Henry said.

Alec sniffed. "Maybe it's closer. I think I can smell smoke."

Henry's lip curled. "Naw, there's nothin'. Just your imagination. Besides," Henry added, "he said they had it under control."

"But embers can be carried a long distance on this wind," Alec said solemnly.

"You won't be givin' me any peace until I get you and the Black and Satan outa here," Henry growled. "Come on, let's go to bed."

They rose and went to the room they shared.

Alec had no idea how long he had slept before he suddenly found himself wide awake. He reached for the clock on the small stand between his and Henry's bed. The luminous dial told him that it was five o'clock, and he knew he had another half-hour before the alarm would go off. It would give them enough time to eat breakfast and still be at the barn before daylight. They'd be well on their way before the others even reached the barn.

Alec lay back on his pillow again. He'd go to sleep if he

could, for there was no sense disturbing Henry's rest. He had closed his eyes when he first became conscious of the smell of wood smoke in his nostrils. Suddenly remembering the northern fire, he sat straight up in bed. He sniffed again. Henry couldn't say he was just imagining this! He smelled smoke with every breath he took!

"Henry!" Alec shouted at the top of his voice. He jumped out of bed and began shaking his friend.

Startled, Henry sat upright. "Eh? Uh. W-what's the matter, Alec?"

"Smoke! Let's get out of here!"

Henry sniffed quickly, then threw the covers off.

Alec tossed Henry's pants to him while pulling on his own. "I looked out the window but couldn't see anything," Alec said. Their room faced east.

"Might be the smoke from that other fire just coming down wind," Henry said, pulling on his clothes. "After they'd put it out," he added quickly.

They were out in the hall when Mr. Ramsay and Tony opened the door of the next room. They had their clothes half on. "You woke us, Alec. Where do you think it's coming from?"

"We're goin' to see," Henry said, running to the stairs. "You'd better wake up the manager of this place."

Alec was following Henry down the stairs when the door of Jim Neville's room opened and the newspaperman shouted after them.

Outside the inn the smell of wood smoke was very distinct. And to the west the somber red of fire lightened the night sky.

"The farm!" Alec shouted shrilly. "It's right there, Henry!"

"Behind it!" Henry shouted. "Get the keys to your father's car, Alec!"

The boy was running back toward the steps when Jim Neville came out the door. "We'll use my car, Alec. C'mon!"

Reaching Jim's car, all three squeezed into the front seat and the columnist quickly drove away. They sped down the main street, then turned left onto the blacktop road.

When they reached the bridge, Jim Neville said grimly, "The wind is coming from the west, bringing the fire right toward us. The rangers will be able to stop it when it reaches the valley."

But for Alec there was no solace in Jim's words. Directly ahead the sky was becoming brighter and in the path of the sweeping wind-driven fire was the state farm. "Faster, Jim!" he shouted. "We've got to get there before the fire!"

"Got her down to the floor now," was all Jim said.

They came off the blacktop road and onto the dirt without slackening speed. They could see the smoke before the fire. . . . It was moving, waving, drifting all about them.

The woods closed in upon the road and the air became soft and warm as they traveled closer toward the heart of the fire.

"It hasn't reached the barn yet," Henry cried. "I'm sure it hasn't! Hurry up, Jim! We're going to make it!"

Bouncing, swaying, the car tore down the dirt road, and when they finally came to the left turn leading to the farm, they could actually hear the roar of the fire.

And when they reached the farm they saw it! From the dark pine forest behind the barn came the roar of wind and fire. Flames reached out amid the treetops, grasping, devouring everything in their path.

But the gazes of the three in the car left this blazing line of fire for the barn. Out of the door, one by one, came the horses!

"The vet and his men must be in the barn!" Henry shouted. "They're driving the horses out of there."

Phar Fly was the first horse out of the barn and, galloping, he went directly to the open gate leading into the field. Avenger followed him, and closely behind came Cavaliere, Sea King and Kashmir.

"But they can't get out that way!" Alec yelled as Jim brought the car to a stop. "They'll be cornered by the fire there!"

Alec was out of the car and running toward the barn when Satan galloped through the doors, his nostrils dilated and snorting in the smoke-filled air. Alec called to him, but the burly colt bolted and followed the others into the field.

"Satan! Satan!" Alec screamed at the top of his voice.

The boy turned back to the barn to find Napoleon coming through the door. Desperately he attempted to head him off, but the old gray swerved away from him to join the others in their run down the long field from which there was no escape.

When Alec stepped inside the barn a heavy bay horse came directly at him and the boy recognized the second test horse. Catching him by the halter, he held him until Henry joined them. "Take him to the road, Henry!" The boy ran into the barn.

The smoke was denser there than outside, and the roar of the fire was almost upon them. He made out the forms of the veterinarian and his men at the Black's stall. Then the door opened and, screaming, the stallion plunged from his stall and came down the corridor.

Alec flung himself at the Black's head when the stallion swept by. His fingers found the halter and held it, but there was no slackening of the Black's stride and Alec was pulled along the floor.

And at that moment the fire reached the barn.

Fire, Added Starter!

17

Just outside the door the Black came to an abrupt stop and Alec heard Henry shout, "Let go! I've got him. Get to the car! Quick!"

But Alec's hand remained on the stallion's halter while he struggled to get to his feet. The veterinarian and his men ran past and, looking back, Alec saw the roof of the barn already engulfed in flames. Behind the barn and as far as he could see everything was a blinding spectacle of white and golden fury, and his eyes blurred as he looked upon it.

Acres of dry forest had been devoured by the flames, and now the strong wind was carrying the line of sweeping fire to the men. The air was alive with tiny particles of fire, and Alec's face smarted and stung as he hurried along beside the Black toward where Jim Neville was waiting in the car. The veterinarian's car sped down the road with the men shouting back for them to hurry still faster.

Suddenly the stallion half-reared, simultaneously whistling his ringing blast of hate and menace. Turning to the field, Alec saw the racers coming in a group around the bend. For a moment he thought they were running for the gate and the road, but then they turned, galloping back down the field at sight of the fire. Frantically Alec called to Satan, but the burly colt moved away with the others.

The Black whistled again, and this time a shrill neigh answered his challenge! It was then that Alec saw Napoleon move away from the upper edges of the field. The gray horse stood still, undecided whether or not to follow the racers.

Shaking his disheveled head, the Black whistled again.

Henry held him firm, trying to pull him toward the road. "Hurry him up, Alec!" he shouted. "We've only got a few minutes before the fire reaches the road, then there's no getting out!"

Alec moved the Black faster, but his eyes remained on Napoleon. Suddenly, around the bend of the field Satan appeared again, running alone! His giant black body moved uncertainly as he swerved abruptly in one direction, then another, seeking escape from the fenced field.

"Satan! Satan!" screamed Alec. If only his colt would go to the gate and if Napoleon would follow him! They still had time before the fire reached the road!

But Satan turned away from the gate once he felt the terrible onslaught of heat. Screaming, he bolted toward Napoleon. And when he swept past the gray, Napoleon whinnied and followed him down the field.

"No! No! No!" Alec cried hysterically.

"My God! Move, Alec. Move! We can't help them!" Henry was pushing Alec, trying to move the boy and stallion past the car. "Let him go in front of us," he shouted. "We'll run the car behind him!"

But the boy turned his head to look once more at the sweeping line of fire racing through the pine tops, sweeping across the grass. The barn was gone, the dry grass before the barn was already afire; in a matter of seconds now the gate would be closed forever to the horses. And then the fire would sweep through the trees surrounding the long and narrow field; the horses would be ringed by flame and driven to their destruction! Was this the horrible fate that was to befall all except the Black? Could he do nothing for them . . . for Satan, for Napoleon?

Suddenly, the Black uttered another terrifying blast. Alec saw Napoleon standing alone at the curve in the field. But the gray came no closer. Now there was no need; he couldn't reach the gate before the fire. *There was no way out.*

"Let the Black go now, Alec!" Henry yelled simultaneously with Jim Neville's shout of warning from the car. But the boy still held on to the Black's halter, while Henry attempted to pull him away. "We can't do anything for the others, Alec! We can't! We can't!"

As though in added emphasis to Henry's shrill cries, the treetops beside the road bent low before the flames, sparks needling the air like thousands upon thousands of fireflies. The raging inferno was reaching out for them in great and terrible leaps.

Jim Neville had the car moving behind them, while Henry continued to tear furiously at Alec's hands to make him let go of the Black. Screaming, the stallion rose, pulling Alec away from Henry. The boy held on, turning him to the side of the road. Desperately, Henry reached out, then cried,

"Alec! Alec!" . . . for the boy had turned the stallion all the way around. He was running beside the stallion, he was flinging himself on his horse. *Alec was going back.*

Henry ran after him, tripped on the bumper of the car and fell to the ground. When he recovered his feet, Jim Neville had him by the arm, pulling him toward the car. The columnist was shouting to Henry, but his words were lost in the tumult of the fire. The air about them was aflame when Henry found himself inside the car. He tried to open the door, but Jim Neville held him and pressed his foot hard on the accelerator. When Henry broke Jim's grasp, he looked back to find the fire already across the road. He slumped limply in his seat, his large hands covering his face.

Alec hid his head in the Black's mane to avoid the flying sparks and heat as he went back. He held the stallion to the road only long enough for the Black to quicken his strides, then he turned him to the fence. The stallion never challenged Alec's guiding hand; he saw the fence and his strides lengthened. It was high, but the boy knew his horse could jump it. He touched the Black, then let him alone. There was a gathering of mighty muscles, then a sudden lurch and Alec moved his body forward with the stallion.

The Black came down lightly on the other side of the fence and was again in full stride before Alec moved his head back from the straining neck. They were in the field with the fire behind them! There remained a way out for the horses, but the Black would have to beat the flames! Alec saw Napoleon standing at the bend in the field, but he turned the stallion away from the gray, taking him closer to the edges of the field. For it was here, somewhere, that he had seen the vine-covered gate and the forest lane beyond. It was this he had so suddenly remembered when he had thought there was no escape for the trapped horses. It was the hidden gate that had brought him back.

Just before the bend he reached it, and brought the Black hard against the wooden bars. They held in spite of the stallion's weight and Alec reached down, taking precious seconds to pull the bars loose from the posts and clinging vines and let them fall heavily to the ground. He saw the lane beyond, while he turned the Black away from it. Now he wished he knew whether it went to the valley, to the road, or to the feared dead end. How he regretted never having walked down it, just once, during all his time spent at the farm. For their lives, his and the horses', now depended on what was at the end of this forest lane.

Napoleon neighed wildly when he saw the Black approaching. But the gray stood still before the heat of the fire and let the stallion come to him. Pulling up beside Napoleon, Alec grabbed his halter and moved him toward the gate. The gray fought Alec as the heat became more intense; the woods on either side of the field were afire as was the dry grass only a few hundred yards above the gate.

Alec held Napoleon until they reached the gate, then he let him go, slapping him hard on his haunches. But there was no need to urge the gray to greater speed, for now he saw the open lane before him and, plunging forward, he galloped down it.

The Black wanted to follow Napoleon, and for a second Alec hesitated. Already the forest lane ahead was alive with pinpoints of light that preceded the flames. Behind him, ever louder, came the terrible roar of fire and wind. He didn't turn to look at it again. His ears told him of its nearness. A

few minutes more and this lane too would be closed by fire.
Would he have time?

He was whirling the Black away from the gate even as he
asked himself this question. For Satan was with the others.
And Satan was his colt. *He wouldn't . . . couldn't . . . leave
him behind.*

Alec goaded the Black to greater speed in the run for the
bend in the field. As the stallion rounded it his strides
lengthened, and Alec knew there was no need to urge the
Black to go faster now. For the stallion had seen Satan as the
burly colt moved across the end of the field to a far corner.
Running before Satan were the others, terrified and bolting
in short, frantic bursts of speed, first in one direction, then
another, seeking escape and not finding it.

In full gallop, the Black uttered his shrill, piercing challenge. It was filled with hate and defiance, and Alec knew
that temporarily the great stallion had forgotten the fire at
sight of the stallions. Urging him on, Alec pulled the mad-
dened horse toward Satan in the far corner, for his plan was
to drive them along the fence up to the open gate.

Even here, several hundred yards before the fire, the air
was hot and it stung his face and eyes. He wanted to close
his eyes, but couldn't . . . for now the Black was rapidly
bearing down upon Satan, and his one intent was to *kill.*

A few strides away from Satan, Alec sat upright, waving
his arm and shouting at the top of his voice. For a fraction of
a second Satan stood still, undecided, then he broke, running
behind the others along the fence.

Swerving, the Black went after him, but Alec pulled him
toward Cavaliere, who was trying to break away from the
group. The Black screamed and turned upon the brown stal-

lion. Alec felt the fury within the great black body, yet he would have done nothing to quell it had he been able to do so. For it was only the Black's hatred for the other stallions and their fear of him that would make it possible to drive them back toward the gate.

The racers broke their tight group when they felt the increasing heat of the fire. They bolted away from the fence and Alec turned the stallion after them. Avenger broke farthest away and Alec headed him off, turning him up the field.

The Black swerved sharply in his desire to reach Avenger, and Alec lost his balance; his hands grabbed frantically at the long mane, holding on to it while he regained his seat. He knew that he never would have caught the Black again had he fallen off.

The racers were running along the fence once more, and Alec kept the Black a little behind and outside the group. The air was becoming too hot to breathe. His throat was tight; he couldn't swallow. The roar of the fire became so great that even the thunderous hoofs racing across the ground could not be heard.

The Black screamed. It was not a scream of haughty defiance and challenge now, but of terror and fright.

They were very close to the gate when Alec saw the burning grass before it . . . a short line of fire that had been ignited by the flying sparks. They would have to cross it to reach the lane!

The racers swerved away to the left, but Alec drove the Black into them. Screaming, the Black forgot his terror of the fire with the impact of heavy bodies. For a few seconds there was an onslaught of thrashing hoofs and raking teeth as the frantic stallions fought one another to get away.

Alec continued pulling the Black's head, directing his attention from one stallion to another. Suddenly Alec saw Sea King's gray body bolt from the group and with a quick jump clear the line of fire. Avenger followed Sea King, and, goading the Black, Alec drove the stallion back against the others. Phar Fly saw Avenger go through the open gate and with a sudden burst of speed he, too, jumped the fire. Cavaliere and Kashmir were next to follow, leaving Satan alone to meet the Black's furious attacks.

Satan rose high on his hindlegs and the Black went up to meet him. Alec felt the terrible impact of heavy bodies as they met. He was losing his seat when the stallions came down. The Black was moving forward again to renew the fight when suddenly Satan whirled and, leaping over the burning grass, went through the open gate.

Screaming in fury, the Black followed him.

The cry of hope which Alec uttered as soon as the Black followed Satan down the lane came to an abrupt end. For ahead he saw that the tops of the trees were already aflame! The lane below was still clear, but it would be only a matter of seconds before it, too, became an inferno.

Satan was running with giant strides in his effort to overtake the other racers more than a hundred yards ahead. All were running wild, their hate and fear of the Black gone with the flames that swept above them.

The ground all about Alec was being engulfed by lashing, leaping flames. And their roar was so great that the boy heard nothing . . . only silence. It was unreal. It was a dream . . . a nightmare. Even the horses ahead were but ghostly apparitions, phantoms floating through the dim, murky veil of heat.

Yet beneath him worked the tremendous muscles of the

Black as the stallion reached out with great strides and extended head. So he knew this had to be real . . . this race with fire.

Snorting, the Black stretched out, but he did not gain any ground on Satan. Alec did not goad him to greater speed, knowing full well that the giant stallion had not reached his limit and would rise to it when it suited him.

They were racing the fire . . . not Satan or Phar Fly, Sea King, Avenger, Cavaliere or Kashmir. That the Black should keep ahead of the flames was all that mattered. Fate had decided that this was the time and the place for the great race. . . . Yet Fate had willed too that their swiftest opponent would be an added starter . . . this wind-driven, all-engulfing fire. And upon the speed of the horses depended their very lives!

Suddenly a deafening roar exploded directly overhead. Flaming tongues and spires dropped all about them. The stallion leaped forward in terror and Alec glanced back to see the white, seething flames swallowing the lane directly behind them and coming forward with inconceivable swiftness.

Terrified, the Black was reaching his utmost speed. No longer was he running Satan down to kill him; hate and menace for the others were gone, leaving only frenzied fear of the flames which sought to devour his straining body.

Racing the wind that drove the fire upon them, the Black followed closely behind Satan as the burly colt bore down upon the others. Together they were outracing wind and fire and overhauling the fastest racers in the world!

But suddenly the lane swept sharply to the left, almost doubling back, retreating into the path of the fire! Alec

heard the agonized screams of the horses in front as the heat
and flames burst upon them. The air was filled with flaming
pine cones and branches, searing and burning as they struck
glistening bodies.

The Black screamed and his strides slowed before the inferno ahead. But there was no turning back and he followed
Satan.

Paralyzed with fear, Alec watched the racers ahead. For as
long as they kept going the lane was still clear. If they
stopped it meant the end for all.

Abruptly the lane turned again and Alec shouted hysterically when he saw the horses move away from the path of
the fire. The Black followed Satan around the turn and ahead
the lane was clear once more except for the canopy of leaping flames above. To their left Alec saw the dirt road, running parallel with the lane but inaccessible because of the
trees. He knew the valley couldn't be more than a half-mile
away now!

The Black screamed again as a burning pine cone struck
his rump, and he surged forward at greater speed. A few
strides ahead, Satan had caught Cavaliere and was passing
him. The Black drew alongside and for a second the brown
stallion kept up with him, then fell behind.

Satan was bunched with Kashmir, Sea King and Phar Fly,
with Avenger running a length ahead, his small body leveled
out, almost touching the ground.

Alec looked behind to see the flames bright behind Cavaliere; then he turned ahead again.

The Black drew closer and closer to the small group, and
just as he moved upon them Satan pulled ahead, moving on
toward Avenger. Straining bodies rose and fell beside Alec as

the Black moved past them, following Satan.

Suddenly the Black uttered a terrifying blast and Alec felt the stallion gather himself. His giant strides came faster. He passed Avenger, then moved up on the burly colt.

It was then that Satan screamed, too, and for a moment Alec thought the colt was going to turn upon the Black. But instead he leveled out still more, keeping ahead of the stallion. Stride for stride they thundered, straining for every bit of speed within their great bodies.

Then Alec, too, let out a cry, for ahead he saw the break in the forest and the rolling, open fields of the valley! They had beaten the fire, outraced the wind! He turned back once more to the racers. They would make it . . . all of them! Cavaliere was closest to the flames, but the fire wouldn't catch him. They had only a hundred yards to go!

A hundred yards.

Alec turned to the open fields ahead, then to Satan's heaving body beside him. Neck for neck, the Black and his colt were racing. Bending low, Alec pressed his head close to the Black.

Both horses screamed again as their nostrils caught the clear air of the valley. Satan's ears were back and flat against his head as he pushed his nose in front of the Black. But then, in one mighty surge, the stallion began moving ahead. Inch by inch he moved past Satan until the colt's extended head fell back to the stallion's hindquarters. And the Black was more than a length in front of Satan when they broke from the forest and hurtled down the slope to the safety of the valley floor.

Hopeful Farm

18

Henry's gnarled hands were clasped firmly about the wheel as he kept the van close behind Mr. Ramsay's car. He sat heavily in his seat with his round bull head slouched down between hunched shoulders. During the six hours they had been on the road he had talked little to Alec, yet very frequently he had looked at him, carefully studying the boy's face before turning back to the road. Alec's eyebrows and lashes had been singed close and his hair cropped even shorter by the fire; his face showed several red blotches where sparks had struck. But only his hands had required attention and they had been bandaged by the doctor.

If the boy was conscious of Henry's continued scrutiny, he did not disclose it. Most of the time he had his head out the van window, always answering Tony's waving hand from the car ahead and turning to the rear to watch the van carrying Satan.

"Just a few more miles now," Alec said excitedly when

they turned off the main highway, following Mr. Ramsay's car up a steep hill.

"Yep," Henry said, shifting into low gear. Once more he turned to look at the boy, and this time he said, "You're sure you don't want to tell me any more about the fire, Alec?"

Shifting uneasily in his seat, the boy asked, "What more is there to tell, Henry? I found the lane and thank God it led to the valley. Satan and the Black are with us. . . . We're going home."

Henry glanced into the rear-view mirror before saying quietly, "Sure, I know, Alec. And that's all that matters. But . . ." He paused, undecided, then continued, "Well, it's just that I caught a glimpse of you during the fire. That was when you neared the road. We were up ahead an' I couldn't see much before the forest closed in on you again. All that mattered then was that you and the horses were out in front of the fire. It's still all that matters," he corrected himself hastily. "But while we've been driving I got to thin-kin' that maybe the International Cup race took place after all." Henry paused. "I guess you're the only one who could answer that," he concluded without taking his eyes from the road.

Alec was silent, while behind him the Black struck the side of the van and Napoleon whinnied.

" 'Course you don't have to talk about it if you don't want to," Henry said slowly.

Turning to the small window in the back of the cab, Alec reached through to put a bandaged hand on the stallion's muzzle. "What do you want to know, Henry?" he asked.

His friend turned to him, and Alec saw the tiny pinpoints of light in Henry's gray eyes.

"Satan was behind the others, when I saw you. Did he catch any of them, Alec?"

"He did, Henry."

"Then you think he could've beaten them in a race. Is that right, Alec?"

"He did beat them, Henry," Alec returned quietly.

"Y'mean he made up the whole distance?"

Alec nodded.

"I knew he could do it," the trainer said proudly. "I just knew he could! But then his face sobered and thoughtfully he turned to the rear-view mirror to glance at the van carrying Satan.

Watching him, Alec knew what Henry was thinking. *Had the Black gone up with Satan? Had the Black possibly beaten him?* The boy understood Henry's glory and pride in the burly colt he had grown to love. And now the fear of defeat was very evident in the old trainer's face.

It was a long while before Henry asked hesitantly, "Was the Black able to catch 'em, too?" His face was tight-lipped, intense.

"Yes, he did," Alec returned slowly.

After a long pause, Henry said, "It was a lot to ask of him, carrying your weight." The trainer turned again to the rear-view mirror and his heavy jowls worked convulsively as he added huskily, "Too much of a handicap to expect him to catch Satan as well." He turned to the boy. "Not a colt like Satan."

Alec raised his eyes quickly to meet Henry's gaze. Without hesitation he said, "No, Henry . . . you couldn't expect that of him."

Henry's heavy jowls relaxed; his tight lips parted in a smile. "We've got the finest horses in the world, Alec," he said almost in awe. "They don't come any greater than those two. We know that now."

They followed Mr. Ramsay's car to the summit of the hill, with Henry talking excitedly of their plans for the future and the colts to come. But for a moment Alec sat back in his seat, content in the knowledge that he alone knew of the Black's superior speed. No, you couldn't expect the Black with such a handicap to catch Satan. *But he had!*

From the top of the hill they could see the valley below, set like a gem amidst the rolling, open countryside. But then they started down, and the evergreens curtained the valley from their sight.

Reaching the bottom of the hill, they followed the road across cleared fields. A wide stream cut the valley and they crossed it by going through the wooden shed of a covered bridge. On the other side they turned right, following the stream.

"We've got to get some mares," Henry said abruptly. "They're as important as having a great stallion like the Black. A sire is only half, remember that."

"We won't buy any until we're sure we have the right ones, Henry," Alec said.

"An' all our colts aren't going to be Satans, y'know," Henry continued. "We'll have hard times in this business, Alec. It's not goin' to be easy."

"I know that, Henry," the boy returned. "But it's what we both want, isn't it?"

"It's that, all right," Henry said.

They came to a white board fence running parallel with the road and turning to sweep far across the fields. Henry smiled, and Alec said to the Black, "You're home, boy!"

When Alec had settled back once more in his seat, Henry asked, "I wonder if you'd do me a favor?"

"Sure, Henry. You know I will."

"I had a letter from an old friend a while back . . . his name is Jimmy Creech." Henry paused. "Jimmy's been racing horses for over forty years. He's a grand guy, Alec."

"Is he a trainer?"

"Well, that and more, Alec. Y'see, he races harness horses. . . . He won the Hambletonian once. Jimmy wasn't content to be just a trainer like me. . . . He wanted more than that; he wanted to take an active part in the race. So he went into harness racing forty years ago, like I said, an' he's still at it." Henry smiled. "A state or county fair wouldn't be anything without havin' Jimmy Creech sittin' in the sulky driving like the devil he is."

"But what do you want me to do, Henry?" Alec asked curiously.

"Things haven't been goin' too well for Jimmy the last few years. He's been sick off an' on, and hasn't been able to race much. He's just about broke. But in his letter to me he said that he'd held on to his best mare an' that he was going to spend all the money he had left breedin' her to as good a stallion as he could get this winter." Henry turned to Alec. "I was thinkin' that maybe we could do him the favor of breeding his mare to the Black. I'd sure like to do it for him. But it's up to you," he added.

"I'd like to do it for him, too," Alec said quickly. "Write him and tell him so, Henry."

Mr. Ramsay's car turned off the road, coming to a stop. Tony got out of the car and opened the wide gate. Before them stretched the entrance to Hopeful Farm, with all its great expectations of things to come.

They drove down the tree-lined lane toward the small stone house at the end. But the eyes of Alec and Henry were fastened on the long red barn set far to the left of the house.

The Black neighed shrilly and Alec turned to him while Henry said, "No more racing days for him. From now on it's his colts who will do the running. And may they all take after him."

The stallion shoved his muzzle through the small window, and Alec pressed his cheek hard against him.

ABOUT THE AUTHOR

Walter Farley's love for horses began when he was a small boy living in Syracuse, New York, and continued as he grew up in New York City, where his family moved. Unlike most city children, he was able to fulfill this love through an uncle who was a professional horseman. Young Walter spent much of his time with this uncle, learning about the different kinds of horse training and the people associated with each.

Walter Farley began to write his first book, *The Black Stallion,* while he was a student at Brooklyn's Erasmus Hall High School and Mercersburg Academy in Pennsylvania. He finished it and had it published while he was still an undergraduate at Columbia University.

The appearance of *The Black Stallion* brought such an enthusiastic response from young readers that Mr. Farley went on to write more stories about the Black, and about other horses as well. He now has twenty-five books to his credit, including his first dog story, *The Great Dane Thor,* and his story of America's greatest thoroughbred, *Man O' War.* His books have been enormously successful in this country, and have also been published in fourteen foreign countries.

When not traveling, Walter Farley and his wife, Rosemary, divide their time between a farm in Pennsylvania and a beach house in Florida.

Life Strategies
for Teens

DAILY CALENDAR

JAY McGRAW

NEW Y

FIRESIDE
Rockefeller Center
1230 Avenue of the Americas
New York, NY 10020

FIRESIDE and colophon are registered trademarks
of Simon & Schuster, Inc.

For information about special discounts for bulk
purchases, please contact Simon & Schuster Special Sales:
1-800-456-6798 or business@simonandschuster.com

Designed by Elina Nudelman

Manufactured in the United States of America

10   9   8   7   6   5   4   3   2   1

Library of Congress Cataloging-in-Publication Data
is available.

ISBN 0-7432-2471-X

Contact Jay McGraw at www.jaymcgraw.com

DEDICATION

I dedicate this book with honor and respect for the fallen soldiers fighting under the banners of the fire and police departments of New York City, Washington D.C., and Pennsylvania. I stand in awe of your dedication, courage, and sacrifice.

And to the men and women of the fire and police departments across America who risk their safety for ours on a daily basis.

Introduction

I have personally lived by and enjoyed the benefits of using the ten Life Laws for many years. I must, however, confess that I am most frequently reminded of Life Law #7, which states: "Life is managed; it is not cured." No matter how well you know the Life Laws or how strictly you intend to live by them, we all need a jump-start—a motivational kick—from time to time. The hardest part of incorporating the Life Laws into your life is overcoming old habits and getting unstuck.

Well, that is *exactly* why I have written this book, *Daily Life Strategies for Teens*—to get the ball rolling and to give you that little kick in the pants that I know I frequently need.

Whether it is motivation, inspiration, or just a quick reminder of what you are looking for, you have found it here. So, have fun with this book, and congratulations for taking that all-important first step toward creating a better life for yourself.

Always remember, work hard and have fun; it's the only way to go.

January 1

"To drift is to be in hell; to be in heaven is to steer."

—GEORGE BERNARD SHAW

January 2

What are Life Strategies? Simply this: Plans for obtaining the things that matter to you in life.

January 3

Knowing what you *don't want* in life is important because that makes it easier to identify the things you want to eliminate from your life.

January 4

Ask yourself these questions every morning while you're contemplating getting out of bed:

"What do I want?"

"What is it I want to do in order to make my life better?"

"What is it I want to do to feel that I'm living with some passion and some kick-ass excitement?"

"What do I want to add to my life?"

"What do I want to eliminate?"

January 5

Do you think you've got the power to make big changes in your life to get what you want? Or do you think that because you're not yet self-supporting and on your own that you're pretty much stuck with what life gives you? I promise you, you've got a lot more personal power than you realize. You just aren't yet aware of how to use it.

January 6

You cannot "cram" for life.

January 7

Everything you will ever be, you are now becoming. It's okay to live in the moment, but the choices you are making now are the building blocks for where you will be later.

January 8

In order to get what you want now and set yourself up for what you want later, you have to take charge of the things that you can influence, and you have to stop whining about the things you cannot. Start thinking about which are which.

January 9

We can bloom where we are planted. We can make our lives work right where we are.

January 10

Being a success and being a winner don't just happen. But you can make them happen if you *know the rules* and learn to play by them.

January 11

You are in control of your life in many ways you aren't yet even aware of. If you understand and use the Ten Life Laws every day, you will receive the level of trust and independence you think you deserve. You will reach that point of self-confidence at which you will no longer be nervous around anyone in your life. You'll know that you'll have the inner strength to handle any predicament. You'll know that you have the tools to make the right choices to get the results you want.

POWERING UP

January 12

"The secret to success is to know something nobody else knows."

—ARISTOTLE ONASSIS

January 13

The Life Laws are in effect 24/7. When you violate these Life Laws, you very simply get what you don't want, and you don't get what you do want.

January 14

There is nothing more frustrating than trying to play a game when you don't know the rules, you don't know the objective, and you don't have the skills that you need to be good at the game. But everything is easy when you know how the game works. Life, in many ways, is a series of games that have rules and skill requirements, just like any other game.

January 15

If you are gong to win the game of life, you have to understand the rules of the game. You also have to know the penalties and rewards associated with breaking those rules.

January 16

If you're not in control, then you're probably following the Ten Loser Laws of Life, the laws that make you a passenger in life instead of the driver:

1. You Just Make It Up as You Go Along.

2. It's Written in the Stars.

3. The Devil Made You Do It.

4. Denial Really Is a River in Egypt.

5. Be Patient; Life Will Eventually Deliver.

6. Life Is What It Is.

7. Get It Right Once and You Are Home Free.

8. People Are What They Are.

9. Get Even Through Grudges.

10. Live Lucky.

January 17

If you choose to ignore the Life Laws and stumble along, wondering why you never seem to succeed, you will cheat yourself out of everything you deserve. So take the time to learn the Life Laws, adapt to them, and mold your choices and behavior to them.

January 18

This is the best time possible to develop a life strategy. This is the time of life when you can build the foundation upon which you will launch the rest of your life. This is the time when you can learn the right way to stand up for yourself and learn to stand up *to* yourself.

January 19

Many of us have just stopped dreaming and we now simply react to whatever life deals us on any given day. The problem is, if you have no idea of what you want, if you have no idea of what your life would include and not include, it is almost impossible to make any kind of plan or live with any kind of purpose.

January 20

Here is a promise you must make to yourself: You have to be willing to start wanting again, and that means identifying what it is that will make you happy.

January 21

Are you out of touch with your deepest dreams? The time to start thinking about this is now.

January 22

Here is another promise you must be willing to make to yourself every single day: You must be willing to change.

January 23

When it comes to taking *positive* risks, taking a real chance that can actually cause a significant change in your life, isn't it true that you are resistant to risk and change because either they seem too hard to face or you fear the unknown?

January 24

"You miss 100 percent of the shots you never take."

—WAYNE GRETZKY

If you want to be outstanding—no matter what it is you want to do—then you're first going to have to stand up for yourself. You may find that the person who is truly holding you back is not a parent or a teacher or the world in general. What's holding you back is *you*.

LIFE LAW ONE:

YOU EITHER GET IT, OR YOU DON'T.

January 26

**REMINDER OF WHY YOU SHOULD KNOW
LIFE LAW ONE:**

to be able to discover and use the huge power you have to change your life. Learn how the game is played so you can get unstuck and have more of what you want and need. Stop being ticked off and start winning. Become someone who gets it.

January 27

People who "get it" have eliminated the types of behavior that just don't benefit them in the long run, and they have figured out what it's going to take to get the results they want.

January 28

People who "get it" don't stew over their problems. They don't look for excuses about why they can't get things done, and they don't get angry and pout about how life can be so unfair.

January 29

People who "get it" *do* make the effort to change their lives by accumulating certain information, putting together a plan, and applying the right skills.

January 30

People who "get it" know that it isn't the luck of the draw that determines who becomes successful. They know there isn't much guesswork involved in getting the results that matter— whether those results be good grades, starring roles in anything from a sports team to the drama club, more freedom and independence after school, or even happiness and a deeper sense of peace.

January 31

People who "get it" know there is a kind of system or process that can be used to get ahead of the pack. For them, learning that system is no different from learning to drive a car or ride a bike. They know there is work required to learn how to navigate through life. *They learn how to make that system work for them.*

February 1

Learn the system and then work it. You *will* get what you want.

February 2

Don't choose behaviors that you know will put you at a disadvantage with the rules of the world.

February 3

When it comes to grades, the guys and girls who "get it" in this world know that if they make poor grades, they get a poor level of respect. They know that if they make mediocre grades, they get only mediocre respect. They know that good grades create a level of respect and trust from parents and teachers that they cannot get any other way. They know that good grades lead to more freedom and more responsibility in life.

February 4

When you "get it," it's as if you are the star in the movie of your own life, and you are *making* things happen rather than *waiting* for them to happen.

February 5

To get anywhere in life, to achieve any of your goals—even the most nonconformist ones—you have to figure out the best way to do it. What rules must *you* follow, and what roles must *you* play?

February 6

"There are no shortcuts to any place worth going."

—ANONYMOUS

February 7

Think about how much time you've put into some aspects of your life. You've spent hours mastering video games or sports, or memorizing songs. But you spend little or no time learning the system of life and then working it.

February 8

There's a big difference between just going from day to day barely getting by, versus understanding who you are, how your life works, and how you can take the initiative to design your life.

February 9

Think of what "getting it" will do for you. If you're in the game of life, whether you're currently playing the game at school for grades, or socially for popularity, or trying to land a certain girlfriend or boyfriend, or competing for a part-time after-school job, think of the incredible edge you will have over everybody else if you understand how the game works.

February 10

It's not uncool to say "No, that bothers me" when talking about behavior you don't want or you're not ready for.

February 11

It's not uncool to have a diversity of friends. It's not uncool to get excited about something in your life, to find a passion, and to live with passion.

February 12

Even if you prefer to march to your own drummer, you still have to interact with other people. If you want to get anywhere at all, you must understand people if for no other reason than the fact that you can get them to do what you want them to do. When you "get it" about other people—when you realize what drives their behavior—then you can use this knowledge for yourself and for your own strategy to be successful.

February 13

Think, for these next ten days, about some of the most common characteristics of all people. If you understand these common traits, it can help you know how to deal with people and be more effective. Here's the first characteristic: Even when it's not Halloween, everybody wears a mask. You must look beyond the mask to see the person.

February 14

Even good people have bad days.

February 15

People often do things for reasons other than the apparent ones.

February 16

People like, trust, and believe those who like them.

February 17

People hear only what they understand.

February 18

People prefer to talk about things that are important to them.

February 19

Everybody, including my sweet old Grandma Jerry, approaches every situation with at least some concern about "What's in it for me?"

February 20

People are easier to manage if you are friendly instead of bossy.

February 21

Everyone's number-one need is acceptance.

February 22

Everyone's number-one fear is rejection.

February 23

Failure is not an accident. You either set yourself up for it, or you don't.

February 24

Resolve to find out how you work—
from the inside out. Make yourself a
project.

February 25

"You did what you knew how to do, and when you knew better, you did better."

—MAYA ANGELOU

February 26

You can choose to become one who "gets it." You don't even have to be the brightest person in the crowd, but you *do* have to be eager and tenacious. You have to decide that you will become one who gets it, no matter what. You have to develop a quality of pushing ahead when the going gets tough. You get it by working and trying harder, inch by inch.

LIFE LAW TWO:

YOU CREATE YOUR OWN EXPERIENCE.

February 27

**REMINDER OF WHY YOU SHOULD KNOW
LIFE LAW TWO:**

to solve the mystery of why your role in
this life is what it is. Get the tools to set
it up differently by changing the statement you make to the world in everything you do.

February 28

"This life is worth living, we can say, since it is what we make it."

—WILLIAM JAMES

February 29

Creating your own experience means making a statement to the world—through your attitude and appearance—that is going to elicit the response you want from other people.

March 1

You control the way the world responds to you by the way you conduct yourself.

March 2

Your entire experience in the world is determined solely by how you engage the world. The way everyone reacts to you—from friends to parents to strangers—is a result of the way you present yourself. It's a result of the way you create your self-image.

March 3

You decide which role you want to play in life, and you decide which response you want to receive from the world. You decide:

How you dress
How you talk
What kind of friends you have
What kind of friend you are
Whom you date
Where you hang out
What kind of work ethic you have
Whether your word is good or not
Whether you are a giver or a taker

March 4

You are responsible for the reactions that your choices and behaviors produce.

March 5

"If you don't like something, change it. If you can't change it, change your attitude. Don't complain."

—MAYA ANGELOU

March 6

What do you think your appearance—
your "look"—is saying to others?

March 7

How do you speak to strangers? What do you think is the initial impression you make on them?

March 8

What is your personality like around other people? Are you a giver or a taker? Are you warm or distant?

March 9

What kind of a sense of integrity do you think you convey to others? Are you sincere, or are you a gossip? Are you a good friend, or are you a back-stabber?

March 10

It's time for you to take a good look at the roles you play in life and to decide if those roles are earning you the treatment you want. Are the roles you are choosing helping to create the experiences you really want out of life?

March 11

Never confuse a goody-two-shoes with someone who is genuinely moral.

March 12

Are you using the roles you play to share yourself fully, or are you using your roles to protect yourself from potential hurt?

March 13

"Press on. Nothing in the world can take the place of persistence."
—RAY A. KROC, FOUNDER OF McDONALD'S

March 14

Create a new experience for yourself.
You can do it right now by taking small
steps. If you're sitting at home with a
hundred pounds to lose, or a D average,
or a bad relationship with your parents,
you can start to take steps to get out of
those situations.

March 15

NEVER FORGET THIS:
Whether you like it or not, you are creating your own experience. The only choice you have is whether you create a good experience or a bad experience.

LIFE LAW THREE:

PEOPLE DO WHAT WORKS.

March 16

**REMINDER OF WHY YOU SHOULD KNOW
LIFE LAW THREE:**

to find out where you have become addicted to hidden payoffs that suck you into self-destructive and self-defeating things. Find out what these payoffs are and how to break their grip on you. Learn to work for the healthy payoffs.

March 17

"All men should strive to learn before they die what they are running from, and to, and why."

—JAMES THURBER

March 18

Do you ever feel really guilty because you do things that you know without a doubt could get you in serious trouble, yet you just can't seem to stop doing them? Do you feel horrible because you do things that you know hurt other people, but you still do them over and over? When asked why you do these things, do you respond, "I don't know why I do that," or, "I don't want to do that"? But the truth is that you *do* want to do it, or you wouldn't repeat the behavior. What you don't realize yet is that there is a powerful set of influences that have grabbed you by the throat. These behaviors give you some sort of quick fix—an immediate reward. They're giving you a "payoff."

March 19

If you want to start taking real control over your life and start making better decisions instead of repeating behaviors that you already know are not good for you—behaviors that ultimately ruin your self-esteem and threaten your safety—then you've got to figure out what "influences" are making you screw up so badly. Connect the dots between your self-defeating behaviors and the payoffs you are getting from those behaviors.

March 20

Your job is to discover what is really going on inside you that makes you act angry or rebellious or self-destructive. If you can do that, then you are on your way to breaking the cycle of negative attitudes and behaviors that are holding you back.

March 21

Do you avoid being a top performer in some area of your life because you fear you will then be constantly forced to live up to higher expectation?

March 22

"Only those who dare to fail greatly can ever achieve greatly."
—ROBERT FRANCIS KENNEDY

March 23

Not all payoffs come from dramatic
negative behaviors. Some payoffs come
from more subtle negative behaviors.
Look at this chart to see if you find
yourself here:

NEGATIVE BEHAVIOR	PAYOFF
Shyness	*No risk of rejection if you reach out*
Bad temper	*Tension release*
Sarcasm	*Don't have to show true emotions*
Mediocrity	*No pressure to perform*
Showing off	*Get much-longed-for attention*
Laziness	*Don't have to get involved in life*

March 24

Just by becoming aware of your pay-offs, you'll be able to take a fresh look at yourself and start making more informed and mature decisions. Just by turning the spotlight on this part of yourself that you never look at, you'll also find that you won't be as susceptible to so many negative influences.

March 25

Do you want to spend your life saying you were too *afraid* to make good grades? Are you going to pay yourself with a safety fix when you know what you need to do is to take the risk of performing?

March 26

Think twice before impulsively behaving in a way that doesn't work for you. Look down the road to the long-term consequences. Weigh the pros and cons of things.

March 27

If you control your payoffs, you will start getting control of your life.

March 28

If someone is treating you in a way that you don't like, find his or her payoff for treating you that way and eliminate it. If you do, the person *will* change his or her approach to you.

LIFE LAW FOUR:

YOU CANNOT CHANGE WHAT YOU DO NOT ACKNOWLEDGE.

March 29

To get real, you must quit living in denial so that you can open your eyes to what is not working in your life.

March 30

"You never find yourself until you face the truth."

—PEARL BAILEY

March 31

de-ni-al *n:* hardheaded, stubborn, and immature refusal to be honest with yourself about the stupid, insensitive, self-destructive things you do to jerk yourself around; unwillingness to acknowledge problems because you wish they weren't there; refusal to take ownership in whatever is not working in your life.

April 1

We all fool ourselves about what's really going on in our lives. We also all fool ourselves about what's going *wrong* with our lives. But the moment we do that, we start hurting ourselves. We start to smother our hopes and dreams.

April 2

When you turn to denial, you ruin what might have been a real chance to overcome a problem, and you ruin the solution that might have worked if you had just tried.

April 3

Life is full of obstacles, and they won't get removed or overcome if you pretend otherwise. It's like ignoring a huge speed bump and hitting it at full speed; it wrecks a smooth ride.

April 4

To deny your problems means to lie to yourself about those problems. You lie to yourself in two ways:

1. *you make stuff up that isn't true; and/or*
2. *you leave stuff out.*

Both forms of lying are equally dangerous. Not telling yourself that something is wrong and letting the problem just build is a sure way for it to catch up with you.

April 5

Living in denial means that you are not giving yourself the chance to improve.

April 6

Stop BS'ing yourself! If you've got a problem, admit it! Get real! Pull your head out of the clouds and be honest. You are not a moron; you know exactly what's not working in your life, and you just need to find the guts to face it so you can start changing it. Whatever is bothering you is not going to go away by itself.

April 7

How do you ever expect to change something if it doesn't get on your "to do" list? Lying to yourself is as dumb as going to a doctor who asks if you're having any pain anywhere, and you say no, even though one leg hurts like crazy. What happens? The doctor doesn't treat your bad leg. How dumb is that? You destroyed any chance to get it fixed, so you limp out the office door the same way you limped in.

April 8

If you get jealous and possessive of anyone you ever date, admit it. If you are so convinced that your parents are out to get you that there is no way you can ever get along with them, admit it. If you are lazy and spend every afternoon and evening listening to music or chatting online instead of studying, admit it. If you recognize that you are behaving in dangerous or self-destructive ways, have the guts to admit it—or you will never bring the situation under control.

April 9

"Hold fast to dreams, for if dreams die, life is a broken winged bird that cannot fly."

—LANGSTON HUGHES

April 10

Are you denying some really bad thinking and behavior? Are you putting obstacles in the road to block you from
achieving success?

April 11

Ask yourself: "What am I doing to put myself at risk in my life?"

April 12

Ask yourself: "What am I doing that is keeping me from succeeding?"

April 13

Ask yourself: "How am I sabotaging myself in my relationships with my parents and other adults?

April 14

Ask yourself: "What am I doing to miss opportunities that I should be grabbing?"

April 15

Ask yourself: "What do I need to change about my personality and behavior patterns?"

April 16

"To get nowhere, follow the crowd."
—CHARLIE BROWN

April 17

One of the most common things we deny is the fact that we stop thinking for ourselves and get mindlessly sucked up in the flow of events around us. In other words, we give in to peer pressure.

April 18

If you don't stand for something, you will fall for anything.

April 19

Have you ever awakened in the morning after doing something against your better judgment, looked in the mirror, and said, "How did I let that happen?" Here's how: You denied your own voice, your own values, and you substituted the judgment of some fool for your own.

April 20

People who "get it" *think for themselves,* because when the bad stuff hits the fan, somehow Joe Cool and his buddies never seem to be there to help shoulder the burden.

April 21

Next time you feel yourself getting sucked into doing something you don't really want to do, remember that you might be doing these things with your friends, but when it comes time to pay the price, you pay it alone.

April 22

If you at least acknowledge to yourself that you are being pressured, then you have a huge advantage. You can anticipate and prepare yourself to deal with the situation. You can decide ahead of time what to say to fight off the peer pressure.

April 23

Take pride in the fact that you're not going to let anyone else run your life, that you know who you are, what you want, and that you are true to your values.

April 24

You also live in denial when you fail to admit to yourself that you are not living up to your potential and are not creating something significant for your life.

April 25

When you're in your "comfort zone," you think you're comfortable, but you're not as happy as you could be.

April 26

When you're in a "comfort zone," you're living a life that is not really satisfying but it is too familiar and too easy to give up.

April 27

When you live risk-free, your life consists of little self-confidence and self-esteem; no sense of pride, and no action or initiative.

April 28

Here are some indicators that you may be stuck in your comfort zone:

You're often bored with yourself.

You feel that your accomplishments are pretty worthless.

You think your daily after-school activities are mostly pointless.

You make promises to yourself that you never keep.

You have no goals.

You're a little scared.

You think your life doesn't have much of a purpose.

You never challenge yourself.

Do any of these statements describe you?

April 29

What parts of your personality aren't working?

April 30

What parts of your behavior aren't working?

May 1

What values and beliefs of yours aren't working?

May 2

What relationships of yours aren't working?

May 3

Being honest means seeing the world—and your life—clearly. It's seeing the immediate threats that loom over your life, and it's seeing the potential problems just forming on the horizon.

May 4

Don't get down on yourself because you are admitting you have problems. Just by acknowledging what you're dealing with, you have already turned a corner. These problems don't define you. You just have some work to do. Get excited! For the first time in your life you have a great chance to make changes—all because you are owning up to what needs to be done.

May 5

By showing the courage and commitment to be honest with yourself and to lay out for yourself exactly how things are, you are going to start breaking out of your comfort zone.

May 6

One of the things you have to realize in life is that you don't have to like everything you do. Sometimes you just have to do it.

May 7

Refuse to stay unhappy for another day. Acknowledge what's wrong and then take action to fix whatever problems you are facing in your life.

LIFE LAW FIVE:

LIFE REWARDS ACTION.

May 8

to become a person who makes decisions and acts on them. Stop floating along in the river of life.

May 9

"What you do speaks so loud that I cannot hear what you say."

—RALPH WALDO EMERSON

May 10

BE. DO. HAVE.

You must **be** committed, **do** what it takes, and then you will **have** what you want.

May 11

If you offer to the world purposeless, meaningless, unconstructive actions, the world will respond to you with the same type of reactions.

May 12

"Do or do not; there is no try."

—YODA, IN *STAR WARS*

May 13

"Someday" is not a day of the week. Intentions—or ideas without actions—are your worst enemy.

May 14

People don't care about what you *mean*
to do. They only care about what you
actually do.

May 15

Fantasy is a substitute for taking action.

May 16

Are you fantasizing? Are you spending a lot of time daydreaming? Are you still coming up with excuses about why you haven't taken action? Or have you decided that you are not going to stay in the place where you are for one more minute?

May 17

Measuring your success or failure purely as a function of results means that you measure your life based on what you do and what you get, not on what you think and what you want.

May 18

We live in a world that is constantly keeping score, and like the scorekeeper at our high-school basketball games, the world doesn't care if you meant to do something. The world only cares about what you have, in fact, done.

May 19

Start keeping score for yourself. Start making yourself take action to improve your life and get the things that you want. Nobody will do it for you. *You* have to do it, and you have to start now.

May 20

Planning is great, but doing is better.

May 21

Take action immediately, because throughout your life you will frequently be presented with windows of opportunity. However, those opportunities will disappear, whether you are ready for them or not.

May 22

Life rewards action. Start moving now. No matter how good you look in a bathing suit, the world's not going to postpone tryouts, or summertime, just because you didn't take action soon enough. You will never succeed if you don't at least try.

May 23

It's always easier and safer, though seldom rewarding, to spend your days not trying anything new. It's easier and safer because you are afraid that if you try something new you might fail or be rejected, and if that happened you would be miserable. However, not trying anything new often causes you to be just as miserable as failing at something new would. At least trying something new has the potential to make you happier.

May 24

Decide that you're going to take some chances, and then take action to ensure your success.

❀

May 25

Make a life decision to risk reasonably, risk responsibly—but risk. Let yourself want more, and take the action to get it.

May 26

"Never let the fear of striking out get in your way."

—BABE RUTH

May 27

Your life should be filled with victories and rewards. If you are losing, that means somebody else is winning, so you know that winning happens. It may as well happen to you, but it's not going to happen by accident.

May 28

Imagine yourself volunteering at a homeless shelter, or even asking out on a date that guy or girl you have always had a crush on. Write down three things you have always wanted to do but never acted on.

May 29

Write down three things you can do *today* to make what you wrote down yesterday happen.

May 30

Don't be intimidated if what you want seems like an impossible challenge. Don't let yourself get overwhelmed by anything. It may seem as if your actions are failing, but be persistent.

May 31

Take action today and you will be successful tomorrow.

June 1

Remember: If you do nothing, you will have nothing.

LIFE LAW SIX:

THERE IS NO REALITY,
ONLY PERCEPTION.

June 2

to find out if you have a warped view of your life. Get in focus so you can hit the bull's-eye.

June 3

The interpretations that we make of the events of our lives—and the reactions that we have to them—are all that matters, not the events themselves.

June 4

Our emotions—fear, anxiety, unhappiness, and depression, among others—are based only upon our perceptions of what is happening to us.

June 5

No matter what happens in your life, how you interpret those events is up to you.

June 6

"Whether you think you can or think you can't, you're probably right."
—HENRY FORD

June 7

It's not necessarily the actual events of our lives that shape us, but rather our perceptions of those events.

June 8

Our perceptions are often distorted rather than clear, and self-defeating rather than constructive. Keep this on your mind today as you analyze your perceptions of the people and interactions around you.

June 9

A big question you must always keep asking yourself is whether or not the lenses through which you view the world are clear, giving you a clean and factual view of your life, or whether they are tinted or out of focus in some way.

June 10

Turn your perceptions on their heads today. Maybe your teachers and parents and classmates aren't actually as weird as you think they are. Maybe they don't think you're as weird as you think they do.

What if they like you more than you think they do?

What if you like them more than they think you do?

June 11

"Better keep yourself clean and bright;
you are the window through which you
must see the world."
>   —GEORGE BERNARD SHAW

June 12

Are you seeing the world through the "peer" lenses? Are you evaluating your entire world based on what others think about you? If you feel you have gained peer approval, you feel successful. You're the type who thinks there is nothing more important in life than being accepted by the right group of friends. They are the foundation of your life.

June 13

Do you have the "I'm in love" lenses on? Is everything in your life dependent on having a boyfriend or a girlfriend? Do you measure your self-worth totally as a function of whether somebody else is in love with you or not?

June 14

Are you wearing the "material" lenses? Are you totally tuned into material wealth, and do you focus on what your possessions are, as opposed to the possessions of others?

June 15

What about the "achievement" lenses? Do you measure your self-worth totally as a function of what you have accomplished? Are you obsessed with grades, club and committee membership, and awards or distinctions? If so, there is little room here for evaluating yourself or others on the basis of character.

June 16

When do you use the "authority" lenses? This lens causes you to be totally focused on how you are relating to those in your life who have authority. Unfortunately, you are either obsessed about gaining their approval, or you are equally obsessed with rebelling against their control. Either way, your obsession dominates your every thought, feeling, and action.

June 17

If you are using the "victim" lenses, take it off! This lens causes you to be obsessed with how you are being hurt or victimized by the world. Things are seldom, if ever, your fault, and you tend to believe that the world is out to get you.

June 18

Avoid the "hate" lenses at all costs.
With this lens, you see enemies behind
every tree, waiting to drag you down.
You know that when people say something nice to you, there is probably a
hidden motive somewhere.

June 19

Don't fall into the trap of the "safety" lenses, through which you see life as a place where it's better to be safe than sorry. You never take risks because you don't trust yourself to handle the pain of failure.

June 20

"What are the lenses I use in my life? How do they make my life better? How do they make my life worse?"

June 21

It's not just the way you see that's critical in determining your perceptions of the world. It's the way you talk—to yourself, that is.

June 22

The tapes playing in our heads have huge influences on us. We are with ourselves all day and all night, and if we are always letting the tapes playing in our heads put us down or put other people down, then think of the devastating effect they can have.

June 23

Think today about what tapes are playing in your head concerning the opposite sex, parents, siblings, and teachers. Just how accurate are these tapes?

June 24

You might know a guy who's a jerk, or a girl who's self-absorbed, or a teacher who's cruel, or a parent who won't listen; but a problem arises if you start to use those past negative experiences with others as the basis for the tapes playing in your head. The problem is that these tapes based on the past are telling you what to think about the here-and-now.

June 25

If negative tapes are playing in your head about members of the opposite sex, whenever you approach a potential romantic relationship you will set that relationship up for failure because it never had a chance to survive.

June 26

Even if you think your thoughts are positive, your negative tapes can overwhelm you and prevent you from evaluating your current situation as it actually is. You don't seek new information about what could be happening. All you do is look for information that confirms what you already believe to be true.

June 27

You have to be especially careful about the tapes that you play about yourself.

June 28

The problem is not the *reality* of your life. It's what you're *telling yourself* about your life.

June 29

The obstacles that you can build in your mind with negative tapes are extremely difficult to overcome. Listening to negative tapes about yourself makes you your own worst enemy!

June 30

Evaluate everything in the here-and-now and you will always be open to the possibility of success.

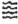

July 1

Tell yourself right now that you no longer have to live with the "interpretation" you have put on your life due to your past.

July 2

Make the decision today to change some of your most damaging perceptions. When you do, your skewed lenses and your negative tapes will soon get tossed aside, and you'll start seeing life from a clearer, more factual perspective.

July 3

Challenge your assumptions. Instead of calling upon all of your stereotypes when you next meet a person, tell yourself that you will evaluate the person as an individual, based on his or her current conduct, values, and beliefs.

July 4

Don't make decisions about your life based on what happened to you last year. Make decisions based on the here-and-now

July 5

It's easy to knock down the obstacles in life with the right kind of inner dialogue. Start talking to yourself the right way.

July 6

No matter what kinds of rules or restrictions are upon you right know, no matter how mean your teachers are, or how little your parents understand you at the moment, or how the world dealt you a lousy hand compared to the rich kid down the street, *you choose how to respond to your situation.*

July 7

You are the voice of your life—not your
past, and not someone else.

July 8

Don't rely only on other people's inspirational voices; you have to rely on your own.

LIFE LAW SEVEN:

LIFE IS MANAGED; IT IS NOT CURED.

July 9

to figure out how to get it going and keep it going. Learn to program yourself rather than simply hope for success.

July 10

"We are what we repeatedly do. Excellence, then, is not an act, but a habit."

—Aristotle

July 11

There is never going to be a time in your life when you will just wake up and be problem-free. The key is to not panic or think you have done something wrong when you do encounter problems. When problems arise, and they invariably will, the first thing you should tell yourself is, "I can handle this."

July 12

We don't need to overdramatize our problems, but making light of them doesn't make them go away; they are still our problems, and that counts. Therefore, they are worthy of our efforts and energies.

July 13

No matter what your problem is, there is a way for you to deal with it if you will just work at it. Successful people succeed not because they don't have problems, but because they know how to deal with their problems.

July 14

Promise yourself that from now on you will make a plan to deal with each new problem rather than to deny or ignore that it exists. Manage your life.

July 15

You have to be your own life manager; you are the only life manager you will ever have. You can't fire yourself if you are doing a bad job; you can only improve on the job you are doing.

July 16

Confront your problems head-on and deal with them constructively rather than create a whole new set of problems due to your reaction—or lack of reaction—to the original problem.

July 17

"Losers let it happen. Winners make it happen."

—Anonymous

July 18

You aren't born a good life manager; you have to learn how to do it.

July 19

Think about yourself as a life manager,
as though you were another self who
had been hired to manage your life.
Pretend that you are calling that other
self in every night for a life management performance evaluation. As you
evaluate this "other self" who is your
life manager, remember that the only
real measure is results.

July 20

Is your life manager putting you in the right place at the right time, or in the wrong place at the wrong time?

July 21

Is your life manager creating your experiences in a way that makes you feel good about who you are and what you are doing?

July 22

Managing your life is not an event; it is an ongoing process. You will never "fix" your life to the point where nothing else will ever have to be done.

July 23

Once you begin to "get it"—once you begin to understand how you can put your life together so that you are in charge of what happens to you—there is a natural tendency to relax. You know you've made some progress, you know you've learned some strong fundamentals from previous affirmations, you know you've developed some new insights into the way you behave. But don't stop working now. Accept that life management is a process.

July 24

I've never seen a winner or a champion who was doing nothing but coasting in life.

July 25

Attaining your long-term goals requires more than willpower and desire. I know this thinking may run counter to what you have heard all of your life. But willpower doesn't work, because it comes and goes; it almost always fizzles out. You need, instead, a *program* that will become a part of your life, a program that will drive you forward whether the emotions are there or not.

July 26

If you want "different," you are going to have to program differently.

July 27

The key to success is perseverance—
getting the job done whether you feel
like it or not.

July 28

Nothing short of setting up your world in a way that is geared to success will get you to where you want to go.

July 29

What you need to do is stop relying on a short-term burst of energy and start creating a permanent lifestyle in which you can't help but change and improve the flow of your life.

July 30

To be consistently successful, you have to put your life-management plan on high priority. I call it putting yourself on "project status." Project status means that it is top priority. It means that you make a specific plan and you commit to it. It means you devote time and energy to succeeding.

July 31

Don't feel selfish about putting your-self at the top of the priority list. If you don't take care of yourself and manage your life, then nothing will get done.

August 1

You can't give away what you don't have. The better you take care of yourself, the better you manage your life, the more you can and will give to others in life.

August 2

When you first begin to manage your life actively, you will initially focus on the things necessary to get you on your feet mentally, emotionally, socially, physically, and spiritually. But soon, as you do a better job of managing your personal life, you will move on to managing the interactive parts of your life, and those around you will benefit greatly.

August 3

A big part of coming up with a strategy for managing your life is knowing who you are and how you feel about some important dimensions of living. You and I have values and beliefs; we just don't talk or think about them much. They are decisions that we have made about what we will and won't do in our lives and what standards we will hold ourselves to. Sometimes it is as simple as personal pride.

August 4

Life decisions take place at the heart level, while daily decisions take place at the head level.

August 5

Becoming a better, more successful life manager means one big thing: making more life decisions.

August 6

What are the life decisions that you can and need to make now that will improve the quality of your life and the efficiency with which you manage it? These life decisions may very well be things that make you require more of yourself than you now do.

August 7

Being a good life manager means, quite simply, getting more of what you want, and less of what you don't want.

August 8

Here are some examples of life decisions that my friends and I have made. They might help you get started with some of your own:

I will not drink and drive.

I will not take advantage of or make fun of people less fortunate than myself.

I will not steal what is not mine.

I will not blame others for my problems or shortcomings.

I will treat people with dignity and respect.

I will live with passion.

I will utilize my mind and my body in positive ways.

August 9

What are five life decisions that you would like to incorporate into your life? These are not casual commitments you are making. These are major principles by which you will always manage your life.

August 10

"The dictionary is the only place success comes before work."

—ANONYMOUS

August 11

Everybody dreams of what might be. It's like going to a movie, but the movie plays in your mind instead of on a screen. It's great entertainment and it can be a lot of fun. But how about turning these dreams into reality? How about making this movie in your mind come true? How about turning those dreams into goals?

August 12

The big difference between dreams and goals is that dreams are kind of fuzzy and vague, and goals are very clear and specific.

August 13

For the next seven days, I am going to walk you through the seven steps that you must take in order to turn your dreams into goals.

HERE'S STEP 1:
Translate your dream into specific events or behaviors that define what you want.

August 14

Translate your dream into things that you can measure.

August 15

STEP 3:

Assign a time line to your goal. ("Some-day" is not a day of the week.)

August 16

STEP 4:

Choose a goal that you can control.

August 17

STEP 5:

Plan a program and a strategy that will propel you to your goal.

August 18

STEP 6:

Define your goal in terms of steps.

August 19

STEP 7:

Create accountability toward the progress of your goal.

August 20

Don't be fooled by all the stories you read about "overnight successes." If you really check out how they made it, you'll discover that they established their goals and went after them the same way you must go after yours: one step at a time, in which a series of smaller goals are accomplished in order to climb to the big one.

August 21

Good life management means *specific* life management. Your goals need to be direct and clear. Keep this in mind over the next four days.

August 22

If you want more dates, then you've got to determine specific ways to manage your social life better. Set specific goals to put yourself at networking gatherings, parties, youth groups, football games, or other activities where you have the chance of forming a relationship. Choose goals that are related to events that you can control. You can't control whether someone asks you out or not, but you can set goals to put yourself in places where you have the chance to be invited. That's what management is all about.

August 23

If you want better grades, then you've got to work on "time management." Set goals to give yourself one extra hour a day for study. If you break down your day to look for that one hour to pull up your grades, then you'll get results.

August 24

If you want to improve your personality, then determine specific ways to manage the parts of your personality that are lacking. If you think you fade into the woodwork too easily, then set specific goals to walk into a classroom, make eye contact, and speak to three people. If you think you are too sarcastic, set specific goals to say something positive to three different people a day.

August 25

If you want to get rid of some destruc-
tive habits—smoking, weekend drink-
ing, casual sex, whatever—then you've
got to manage your way out of them. It
isn't going to be good enough just to
decide to say no. There are going to be
great temptations and peer pressure for
you to stick with your old ways. You
need to have very specific goals about
how to keep yourself out of situations
in which the peer pressure will be intense. You've got to have a plan to be
somewhere else on Friday nights instead of at a party where alcohol is
served. You've got to have a specific
plan to keep you from getting in the
backseat with somebody so that the
chance to have casual sex is far less
likely.

August 26

Managing your life does not mean overnight changes will occur. Changes will come slowly. But so what? There is power in persistence. The philosopher Samuel Johnson once wrote that "great acts are performed not through strength, but by perseverance." And that is true; the simple, small goals are what will transform your life.

August 27

Through life management, as you accomplish each small goal, you will discover that you have even more goals you want to reach. You will wake up every day feeling a passion to get even more things accomplished. You will feel productive and confident in a way you never knew you could feel.

August 28

Managing a life that is a total wreck is a big problem and challenge. But once you get on a roll, once you have momentum, your management method starts to feed on itself and you will love the result.

LIFE LAW EIGHT:

WE TEACH PEOPLE HOW TO TREAT US.

August 29

**REMINDER OF WHY YOU SHOULD LEARN
LIFE LAW EIGHT:**

to start controlling and stop complaining about your relationships. Learn to renegotiate with everyone in your life to get the treatment you want and deserve.

August 30

"Don't make yourself a mouse, or the cat will eat you."

—A. B. CHEALES

August 31

People "size you up" based upon the way you present yourself to the world. Through that presentation, they are deciding what you can bring to their life and what they can bring to yours. They are deciding what they can do for you, and what you can do for them. They are deciding what they can accept from you, and what you will accept from them.

September 1

People decide how to treat you based on their observations of you. They will test you. Based on your responses to their tests, they will either continue their initial way of treating you, or they will change their approach. Do you see what this means? It means that you get to influence their decisions greatly. You can be the one who sets the tone.

September 2

"If you refuse to accept anything but the best, you'll get the best. Begin to live as you wish to live."

—ANONYMOUS

LIFE LAW EIGHT

September 3

If you reward someone's behavior by reacting in a way that he or she desires, you are likely to see that behavior again. If you respond in a way that he or she finds undesirable, you are less likely to see that behavior again.

September 4

Yesterday's lesson also applies to your enemies, particularly when you both occupy the same rung on the social ladder. If someone at school is continually taking unfair potshots at you, you are somehow rewarding that behavior; otherwise, that person wouldn't be so likely to continue the assault.

September 5

If someone at school is trying to hurt you continually by excluding you from a certain group or activity, you are somehow rewarding that behavior, however unintentionally, or that person wouldn't continue it. You have communicated, by word or deed, and taught that person that his or her behavior is acceptable to you.

September 6

You must own, rather than complain about, how people treat you.

September 7

Even if a family sets boundaries and limits that we have to follow, we can have an influence over what those boundaries are. Sometimes, if we are smart, we can get our families to widen the boundaries within which we operate—all because we teach them how to treat us.

September 8

Even if your family is being unreasonable, ask yourself this question: What are you going to do to change the way they treat you? You taught the parent how to treat you. Now all you have to do is teach your family to treat you in a different way.

September 9

RED ALERT!

You are entitled to be treated with dignity and respect. If someone is rude or inconsiderate toward you, that's one thing, unpleasant as it may be. However, if someone is physically, mentally, or emotionally abusing you, that's totally different, and unacceptable. You did not teach anyone to do that! If any of these horrible realities are in your life, get help. You can do so confidentially without exposing yourself to danger. Teachers, clergy, counselors, and other trusted adults will help you.

September 10

You have trained your parents—and the other adults in your life—with your reactions in the same way you train your dog to sit or roll over. Your behavior conditions other people to expect the same responses time after time. How are you conditioning adults to treat you? Does your behavior tell them that if they ignore you, you will just go away, or that you will always cause a problem, or that you will be mature and flexible in your negotiations with them?

September 11

If a parent tells you something you
don't want to hear, and you blow up,
yell, scream, stomp off to your room,
and slam the door, then you have re-
warded a parent's strictness by rein-
forcing his or her perception of you as
childlike and immature.

September 12

Do you go to your parents only when you have some ridiculous question or problem that leaves them with no option but to dismiss or discipline you? When you act like this, you teach them to deepen their perception of you as an irresponsible individual.

September 13

You can also teach people how to treat you by what you *don't* say. For example, you have been out with your friends and come home at the very last moment before your curfew. Your parents confront you and ask what you did and where you went; you are evasive and vague and dismissive. Realize that in situations like this one, you are teaching them to be nervous about what you are doing when you are out. People who have nothing to hide, hide nothing. Are you teaching your parents that you have something to hide and therefore they should be nervous and impose more limitations on you?

September 14

You may not be the one in control in your relationship with your parents, but you have significant ability to get your parents to do more of what you want them to do, and less of what you don't want them to do. All you have to do is change some key actions and re-actions that you throw out to them. This is called "upstream management." Change the way in which you are engaging your parents, and they will change the way they react.

September 15

If you interact with your parents in any of the following ways, it will greatly increase the amount of freedom and respect they give you:

- *Initiate conversations with them.*
- *Don't take the bait; stay calm.*
- *Become interested in their lives, and they will show interest in your life.*
- *Stop demanding and start earning your freedom.*
- *Inspire confidence and trust through predictability.*
- *Allow yourself to be influenced by your parents' advice.*
- *Be easy to get along with.*

September 16

If people, particularly your parents, are at first resistant to changing how they treat you, it is because you taught them to be resistant. You taught them so well that they have formed habits. Habits can be stubborn, but they can be changed. Keep trying.

September 17

If you expect either of your parents to be negative, critical, and resistant to your ideas, that is most likely how you will interpret their behavior, even if that is not how they are actually behaving. To make sure you are delivering the message that you want, you must check your expectations and figure out if you and your parents are setting yourselves and one another up for disaster. Realize that through your behavior you can create new expectations with your parents that get you what you want.

September 18

People learn by the results that you choose to give them, and in that respect you are in control of every relationship you have.

September 19

What have you been teaching your parents? That you are reliable, predictable, and competent? Or that you are going to break and run off every time you get half a chance? Seriously decide what you have been doing to set your relationship up, however it is; and remember, you are not a victim.

September 20

If you are unhappy, you can change
your situation all by yourself; you don't
need active help and cooperation from
anyone else. You can begin making
huge changes in all of your relationships completely by yourself. Simply by
deciding that you will no longer accept
behavior that you do not want, you are
making an important commitment to
change.

September 21

What would it mean to your mother and father, for example, if you simply approached them just to ask about how their days went, when you didn't want anything, didn't need anything, and didn't have a problem to solve? How would it make them feel to know you took an interest in their lives? That would probably cause them to treat you like the adult you were being.

September 22

Your power and ability to change relationships is not limited just to that relationship you have with your parents. You have control over how your peers treat you, as well. Both the good and the bad news is that you have taught or allowed the bully or walking gossip column or fair-weather friend to treat you as he or she does. So you have control over your interactions and you can decide to do something to change them today.

September 23

Make the decision right now that you will not give up and accept treatment that you don't want.

September 24

Your job is to find out what "payoffs" you are creating that maintain the behaviors you don't like in others.

September 25

All relationships can be renegotiated. You can reopen negotiations through either word or deed. To do this you have to identify what you are doing to support and allow the behaviors that you don't like in others. Once you have identified those behaviors, then you start changing to make others change, and people will treat you in a different way.

September 26

One of the strange laws of human nature is that we tend to conform to that which is expected of us. Do people have negative expectations of you and your behavior? What are they? How can you change those expectations through words and actions?

September 27

The most important relationship you will ever have—the one that sets the tone for every other relationship in your life—is the relationship you have with yourself. Everyone in your life will watch how you treat yourself, study what you require of youself, and determine whether or not you are willing to stand up for yourself.

September 28

When you treat yourself with dignity and respect, you send a loud, clear message that you are now in a position of strength and power. You are sending a loud, clear message to negotiate more effectively what you really want.

September 29

"It is not fair to ask others what you are not willing to do yourself."

—ELEANOR ROOSEVELT

September 30

Teach people to perceive you in the way
that you feel you actually should be
perceived.

October 1

If you do not have the conviction in your heart and mind about who and what you are and what you require, you will always be creating more problems than you could ever imagine. You'll be letting people into your life who are not particularly interested in treating you with dignity and respect.

October 2

Remember the principle of reciprocity: You get what you give. You should never expect people to give you something that you are unwilling to give yourself.

October 3

Treat yourself well so others will be motivated to treat you well, too.

෨෧

LIFE LAW NINE:

THERE IS POWER IN FORGIVENESS.

October 4

to set yourself free of the anger, hatred, and bitterness that result from bad treatment. Learn to exercise the choice of forgiveness.

October 5

"Man is free at the moment he wishes to be."

—VOLTAIRE

October 6

When someone hurts you emotionally, the pain lasts long after the actual
event. It can go on for days, weeks,
months, even years. It can diminish
your confidence, your self-esteem, and
possibly change your heart and make
you bitter.

October 7

At this stage in life, there are lots of people above you in the pecking order, and they aren't very sensitive to what you think and feel. There are a lot of people who see life as a fierce contest, and they always want to "one up" you, even if it means back-stabbing you and making you the target of lies, gossip, and other mean and hateful verbal attacks. They hurt you by isolating you and leaving you out of activities in which you want to participate. When these things happen, it's difficult not to hold a grudge, but you must *make the decision not to do so.*

October 8

Consider these questions:

Do you want to think you're right, or do you want to be happy?

Do you want to be a martyr, or do you want to stop being angry every day?

October 9

If you really get hurt, then you'll start withdrawing emotionally. You'll withdraw in one of three ways:

1. You'll live behind an emotional safety wall, keeping yourself away from others so they can't hurt you again.
2. You'll turn sullen and sarcastic, becoming a master of the put-down, thinking that it's better to get others before they get you.
3 You'll become a robot and just won't acknowledge feelings, good or bad.

Have you fallen into any of these traps?

October 10

It's extremely important to remember that carrying fear, frustration, disappointment, and anger within you changes your physical being. It creates a physical imbalance in which you have too much of some things and not enough of others. You may be experiencing sleep disturbance, nightmares, poor concentration, fatigue, and any number of even more serious ailments. This is not okay. It is not acceptable to settle for a silent, private hell. Don't settle for such an existence just because you don't feel worthy of seeking help for a problem or drawing attention to yourself.

October 11

You cannot be happy and sad at the same time; you cannot be peaceful and in turmoil at the same time; you cannot have hope and optimism while you are withdrawn and shut down. You cannot be physically calm and constantly nervous at the same time. However you try to set up your protection, holding on to such anger and pain and resentment exacts a very high price from you.

October 12

Why stay trapped in a lonely, dark prison where it is impossible for happiness, hope, and optimism to grow? Within that prison, you might fly into rages where you fight back, or you'll withdraw emotionally, hoping the hurt will go away. You could try to justify your misery because it was caused by the action of someone else, but really, what kind of life is that for you?

October 13

As long as you are nursing some kind of misery, you are not functioning at your peak. You are still letting a person's attack hurt you.

October 14

"Be your own palace, or the world's your jail."

—ANONYMOUS

October 15

When you've been hurt by someone, as unfair as that is, you must deal with it. Instead of shutting down for the rest of your life, tell yourself that you can break out of that prison and reclaim your place in the world. You may have a right to be bitter and angry, but you have a responsibility not to be.

October 16

When you are filled with bitterness or loathing for someone else, you are locked in a bond with that person. Anger tightens, rather than weakens, your bond with that person.

October 17

If you allow yourself to be full of anger or resentment toward another person, you are allowing that person to continue to poison your life—the way you see the world and yourself.

October 18

Don't allow one person who has hurt you to poison every other relationship you might have or enjoy.

October 19

The door to an emotional prison locks
from the inside.

October 20

You may not be responsible for bad things that happen to you, but you are responsible for handling the situation.

October 21

One of the most difficult decisions in life is the decision to forgive someone who has hurt you deeply. But if you find the strength to forgive and to say "I will not hate you another day. I will not invest my spirit in you another day. I will forgive you so I can be free," you will unlock the door to your prison.

October 22

Anger is a fact of life. It is an emotion that should not be stifled. If you have been wronged, you should feel wronged and you should say so. It's important that you correct someone who needs correcting. But then it's important to do one other thing: to let the anger go.

October 23

When you forgive someone, you thrive despite him or her.

October 24

As good as it feels to hold a grudge and to be righteously angry, overcoming a grudge can be a much, much better feeling. As the old saying goes, "Living well is the best revenge."

October 25

Forgiveness is often all about you, not about whoever has hurt you. Sometimes it does not matter if the other person ever even knows you have forgiven him or her. It does not matter if he or she ever even acknowledges hurting you. You are the only person who has to know about this forgiveness, because this is something that takes place within you and for you.

October 26

Forgiveness is not a gift for the person who has hurt you; it is a gift for yourself.

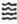

October 27

Will you continue to carry the burden of being wronged by someone else, or will you break out of your personal prison and reclaim your place in the world of happy people?

October 28

Is it fair that you got put into an emotional prison by the person who hurt you? No. Is it easy to get out of it? No. Is it worth it? Yes—because you are worth it.

October 29

If you forgive the person who has hurt you, stolen your boyfriend or girlfriend, or gossiped about you, you are essentially saying to that person: "I will no longer suffer 24/7 because you are a jerk. I'm not going to get filled up with hate when I pass by you in the hall. I'm not going to shut down emotionally anymore, with my teeth gritting and the blood boiling in my veins."

October 30

The world doesn't care that you are angry. You can sit in your room every night angry, bitter, and shut down. But I guarantee you that that won't do one thing to change what is wrong in your life. The world just keeps on spinning around. So understand that you are not helping yourself, and you are not getting sympathy while you suffer.

October 31

Forgiveness is all about *you*, remember. When you forgive someone, you are saying to him or her and to yourself: "You have hurt me enough; I will not take over for you and make sure that I stay miserable by staying angry and ticked off. I am choosing to give me the gift of love."

November 1

You want emotional closure after you've been hurt. You want to be able to say honestly that you have no unfinished emotional business left with the people you have been focused on.

November 2

To be *really* free, you have to *really* forgive.

November 3

Forgiveness is not a feeling; it is a decision.

November 4

Forgiveness is an intellectual choice, not an emotion. This is good news. Fortunately, charitable and forgiving feelings don't have to be in place for you to free yourself from an emotional prison.

November 5

After you've been hurt and you make the decision to forgive, aim for the "I'm out of here" response—that is, do the *very least* that you have to do in order to get emotional closure.

November 6

Right now, figure out who in your life has you trapped in the claws of bitterness and resentment, and then decide how to achieve emotional closure with that person.

November 7

You are not the only one who pays a price when anger, hatred, and bitterness overwhelm you. Those who love you pay a high price, as well. If all of the emotions you have are negative ones due to your resentments and your grudges, then those are the only emotions you can pass on to others.

November 8

You can't give away emotions that you
don't have or that you are not nur-
turing.

November 9

You cannot give a pure love to your girl-friend or boyfriend, or your siblings or your parents, if your heart is full of anger.

November 10

You can't give out quality love to people if you have shut down to protect yourself against pain. You may think that you can hate your parents and still love your girlfriend or boyfriend, but you can't. Maybe you feel that you are escaping into their arms with love today, but as time wears on, deep anger will creep in and poison that relationship. Get those emotions out of your inner self so that all that's in your heart is love, forgiveness, light, hope, and optimism.

November 11

Don't make new relationships pay for the sins and transgressions of those that came before them.

November 12

Make sure you don't contaminate your new relationships by dragging unwanted baggage into them. If you don't reach emotional closure with your previous boyfriend or girlfriend, you're going to let that person continue to control you in your future relationships—control you in every relationship you will ever have. If that is not an incentive to motivate you to want to be free, I don't know what is.

November 13

BOTTOM LINE:

Forgive. Take your power back. You're worth it.

November 14

Forgiveness is a choice to which you are entitled.

LIFE LAW TEN:

YOU HAVE TO NAME IT
BEFORE YOU CAN CLAIM IT.

November 15

**REMINDER OF WHY YOU SHOULD LEARN
LIFE LAW TEN:**

to get dead-on specific about what you
want and find the courage to step up to
what is yours.

November 16

"The indispensable first step to getting
the things that you want out of life is
this: Decide what you want."

—BEN STEIN

November 17

When you say you want to be happy and successful, do you know precisely what that means? Do you know exactly what you want your life to be? You've got to be drop-dead, bull's-eye, dead-on sure of what you want, or you might blow right by it and not even know it's there. You've got to know everything about it. You've got to know how it looks, feels, smells—everything.

November 18

ASK YOURSELF AGAIN:

Are you able to describe specifically
what it is that you value for your life,
and are you willing to work toward that
goal? Can you stand up right now and
declare what you want? Can you name
the very thing you need to feel completely fulfilled? Can you come up with
it? Think hard.

November 19

Winners in life are those who know exactly what they want. They can visualize themselves at the place where they are perfectly happy. They know exactly what they are going to have and who's going to be there to share it when they have it.

November 20

Happy people generally know what they want, and they feel they are moving in the direction of getting it. That's what makes them happy! They feel they are headed for something they love.

November 21

It's easy to complain about what we *don't* want, but it's surprisingly difficult to say what we *do* want. It's time you fix that.

November 22

"You got to be careful if you don't know where you're going, because you might not get there."

—YOGI BERRA

November 23

Other people are convinced they know what they want without thinking very hard about it. They work for years to get where they think they want to go, yet when they finally get there, they realize that it wasn't what they really wanted at all. Had they taken the time to figure things out genuinely, had they been moving down the right road instead of the wrong road, their lives would be completely different.

November 24

You will have a great advantage in life if you learn how to name it accurately—exactly what you want—before you can claim it. So don't take lightly the step of defining your dream. It deserves all of your attention, all of your urgency. You want to be flexible and study all of your options. But don't be lazy and tell yourself that your "dream" should not be taken seriously. Just as you know that you have to sign up in time for cheerleading or football team tryouts, you have to name what you want because people won't wait for you to make up your mind.

November 25

Don't become fixated on some object, event, or activity as the thing that you want, when in reality what you want is the feeling you think that object, event, or activity will give you.

November 26

By refusing to become fixated on an object, event, or activity as the key to your happiness, you give yourself a lot of flexibility. If you identify the *feelings* you need to be happy, you will figure out any number of different ways to get those feelings. If you are open to different experiences, you may find, for example, that you get real feelings of self-respect and pride from being a good friend rather being friendly with famous people. Or you may find that there are hundreds of ways to feel as if you have more freedom or popularity that have nothing to do with what you drive or what you wear.

November 27

Every detail that you can know about your long-range goal in life will help you to get there quicker and more successfully.

November 28

As you go through the process of naming what you want for your life, it's okay to say, "I want this for me." If someone gives you grief about your dreams for the future, don't listen.

November 29

The people who stay stuck are those who refuse to dream.

November 30

It is important to want more in your life and it is important that you make yourself a priority.

December 1

Don't be shy about saying that you want something special for yourself, whether it is a special feeling, a special experience, or a special item. And what's more, don't be shy about working on it, asking for help, and using everything in your power to get your constructive goal.

December 2

Like my granddad always used to say: "You will never catch a fish if your hook isn't in the water." You will never get something you don't ask for. Even if you are just asking yourself for it, you have to ask.

December 3

Once you know exactly what you want, don't forget the second half of this law: claiming what you have named. Knowing what you want is worthless if you are not willing to step up and take it once you have gotten there.

December 4

You have to have the guts to say "This is my destiny." It sounds lofty. But you make it your reality. You say "This is my goal, I am here, I have earned my way to it, and I'm going to take it."

⚡

December 5

Don't let anybody make you feel selfish
or guilty for stepping up and claiming
what you have worked hard to get.

December 6

"I wasn't lucky. I deserved it."
—MARGARET THATCHER

December 7

In claiming what you want and going
after it, you are not stealing anything;
you've earned it and you deserve it. You
have worked hard, applied the Life
Laws, and now it is your turn to step up
and take what you have earned.

December 8

There is a practical reason to stepping up. We live in a competitive world; if you don't take what is yours, somebody else will. Why would you want to make it easier for another competitor? Why leave your windows open for a thief?

December 9

It is time to get going and to lead a life full of challenges, aspirations, excitement, and happiness. It's time to take the journey that you are meant to take. Remember to enjoy the journey.

December 10

As has been said many times, the game of life is not about the final score but about the playing. It's not about the destination but about the trip. If you live life to its fullest, whatever that kind of life is, then you have become a winner. You have become one of those who "gets it."

CONCLUSION

December 11

As far as sex goes, your body is your choice. This choice is a big one and deserves serious, deliberate thought. Remember that you can mess up your life big-time in a hurry if you don't think about the possible consequences of your choices and actions.

December 12

When you choose any behavior, you also choose the consequences. That's the problem with "grown-up" behavior like sex: If it goes wrong, it can go way wrong. There is an old saying: "Every rose has its thorn." Sex is no exception.

December 13

A friend of mine has a T-shirt that sums up pretty well an important point about sex:

Love is fickle, it goes away
But HERPES is here to stay!

On the back it says:

And AIDS will freakin' kill you!

December 14

On the subject of sexually transmitted diseases, what I've said about other areas of your life holds just as true: You create your own experience and you teach people how to treat you. Think that through and see what it tells you about the price being charged against your body. Ugly, but true.

December 15

Sex is your decision, but do yourself a favor by thinking ahead about how you will feel if, in fact, the worst happens and you get pregnant, infected, or dumped. Be honest with yourself. Don't be in denial about a possible downside, because it's real—very real.

December 16

Regarding sex, consider your decision morally, socially, behaviorally, physically, and emotionally. It is not a simple decision, because once you do it you cannot undo it.

December 17

KNOW THIS ABOVE ALL ELSE:

It is your body and you have the right to say *no!*

December 18

If you are doing drugs, that behavior is nuts and you need to quit—and quit *now*. Remember Life Law Three: People Do What Works. Obviously, you are getting some payoff if you are doing drugs. You have to get real and ask yourself what the payoff is: Is it really what you want, or are you hiding from your life? I mean, think about it—can something you swallow, smoke, snort, or inject really fix your problems? No way! You may wish it could, but it can't. Do you think it prepares you for or gets you closer to anything on your goals list? No way!

December 19

We often start or pick up habits for one reason, yet continue them for a completely different set of reasons. If you were doing drugs before you read this book, it was most likely because you were one of those who didn't get it. It was because you didn't have things going on in your life, you had no momentum, no goals, and no plan to get them. You probably started doing drugs because you thought it was a good alternative, and to be honest, you had damn little else on which to focus. Now, hopefully, you are becoming one of those who does get it and therefore you don't need that nasty stuff anymore. You do have plenty going on— like your whole life, for example! You didn't need drugs then; you certainly don't need them now.

CONCLUSION

December 20

Don't continue to do drugs and don't continue to hang out with people who do them. Most people who do drugs in high school do them because it represents for them the easy way to define themselves—it gives them some identity. The only price of admission to that group of losers is doing the drugs. Free pass, it seems, but in fact, a very, very high price is being paid, and you are the one who has to pay it.

December 21

Require more of yourself. Use your inner power and your mind, not some chemical. You are better than that and you know it. When you stop buzzing your brain and start thinking and taking pride in yourself, I'm betting it won't be very long at all before you look back on your "drug days" and say "How dumb was that?"

December 22

You decide how you feel about yourself. If somebody right out of the blue decides not to include you or like you, so be it. Don't give that power to anyone else: not friends, girlfriends, boyfriends, family—nobody.

December 23

Put energy and effort into friendships you would like to have, but don't beat yourself up if someone is ultimately not as interested as you are in exploring that friendship.

December 24

Popularity is not all it's cracked up to be. "Cool kids" are that way only because you and maybe some other people decided to label them as such. They are no different from you. You shouldn't tear them down in your mind and heart, but neither should you build them up.

December 25

If you had a choice between having one loyal, honest, good friend, or ten "cool" kids who might not have those qualities, which would you choose?

December 26

"Everybody else is doing it" is a pretty lame reason for doing anything. Think for yourself. Choose for yourself. You and your friends may do stupid stuff together, but you alone will pay the price for that stupidity.

December 27

If you are caving in to peer pressure to do drugs, have premarital sex, blow off school, defy your parents, or just generally be ticked off because "everybody is doing it," you have stopped thinking.

CONCLUSION

December 28

You are an original. God made one form and then broke the mold. When you think about that, it is really pretty cool. Wouldn't it be a waste if you never, ever actually figured out who you were and never, ever let yourself be that unique person because you were so busy kissing up to somebody else or were caught up in rebelling or defying the authorities in your life to the point that you forgot about being who you really are?

December 29

When you are comparing yourself to someone else, you are comparing your true self to the other person's social mask. You are going to lose that contest 100 out of 100 times. The truth is, others may be going through much more hell than you ever thought about.

CONCLUSION

December 30

Having the only one of anything in this world is pretty cool. And you have the only one of you. Treat yourself as the treasure you are.

December 31

Believe in yourself, be who you are, and don't put yourself down in comparison to other people. You have the potential for a great life ahead of you, but it is up to you to live it.

About the Author

JAY MCGRAW is the author of the *New York Times* bestseller *Life Strategies for Teens*. He is currently enrolled at Southern Methodist University, in Dallas, Texas. He enjoys spending time with his friends and his younger brother, Jordan.